I'm Born a Woman, Not Daddy's Son

I'm Born a Woman, Not Daddy's Son

Irene O. Ogbru

A Geneva Book

Carlton Press Corp. New York

Copyright © 1996 by Irene O. Ogbru
ALL RIGHTS RESERVED
Manufactured in the United States of America
ISBN 0-8062-5159-X

Dedication

To my husband, Dr. Benjamin Ogbru, and the men and women whose encouragements, dedication and support provide role models to fulfill the role of a creative woman.

Also to Paul Lippman, the editor.

Preface

Helen Brown liked to think about her early childhood abandonment as a challenge, with the thrill of a dangerous enemy chase, preparation and mercy to fulfill her role as a woman. Though she was a restless, crying little girl looking for a father's love, it took love, passion and couple's support to complete the role of woman's creation.

Her mother was the only person who could give her the full-time care that she needed. But down deep inside, Helen knew that something else had driven her from men's physical love until Eric found her. She chose to lead a solitary life, and no amount of gentle persuasion could weaken her faith. This is the case of a traumatic event and Helen's need for faith to face her destiny.

While Helen struggled to be educated, her father still could not love her as a woman. She was kind, charming, loving, spirited and incredibly vulnerable because of her beauty. Her sister Judy's role was very destructive, reflecting the true nature of a sister's jealousy.

Despite bold and merciless friends, relatives and the community that never valued education, Helen and Eric together proved the role and value of a good education, and couple partnership.

Helen's dream, seven months after Enoch's death, draws our attention to God's promise sketch plan of the nature of a place of rest for the human kind, "Life After Death." It also proves a wicked soul suffers in hell. Whatever human beings have done on earth waits for the soul.

Helen has the strength, faith and character that fulfills- both roles of God's creation, a man and woman, creation of one flesh.

I'm Born a Woman, Not Daddy's Son

Chapter One

The creation of woman brought a complete meaning to man's existence on earth. Before Eve was made, Adam was a faithful man, but Eve's creation made Adam and Eve a complete Circle. They became the father and mother of all human beings.

Real love grew and became the root to protect and guide Adam and Eve. Intimacy became the first building block of marriage. Marriage became the joy and honor of human life. But the meaning of marriage is changing as time changes. Still, a woman's status changes very slowly.

This is because society believes culture is the root of civilization and civilization gave birth to modern times, while modern times try to heal a woman's pain like Helen Brown's childhood pain and fears that hurt her.

One of Helen Brown's strongest childhood memories still causes her tremendous pain. This feeling always flashes across her mind.

She was the second child and the second daughter. Her father, Enoch Brown, visited his wife, Rebecca, in the hospital and huffed, "Another girl, Rebecca?"

Rebecca looked at him and didn't say a word.

*Sweet Mother and Baby.
Mother wrapping baby in her arms
as Enoch walked away from the hospital.*

Enoch cried out loud, "Oh, God, why am I being punished? I'm the first child and first son of my father. Why am I doomed?" He ran away with tears in his eyes, and he was very emotionally disturbed. He denied the truth that the baby was a female.

His hands shook, and he shrieked. He stood and screamed out loud, "She can't be a woman! Take her Rebecca, she is yours." He intentionally denied her for being a girl.

Two neighbors came into the room and said, "Enoch, next time, she can give you a son." They cried and said, "Enoch, the baby will have a better future. You will live to see what the baby will become in your lifetime."

Enoch stared at the baby and got angry. He started fidgeting and hitting himself with his hat, and, at the same time, talking like the end of his life had arrived.

Rebecca watched Enoch pour out his anger and frustration, then she said, "Oh Lord, she is my baby. I love her." She lifted the baby and gave a Prophet to Enoch.

Enoch looked and said, "Woman, you don't understand. She can't be a woman. Don't tell me she will be intelligent and beautiful. Oh yes, my name is lost forever."

Dorothy, their neighbor, said, "The baby is your daughter."

He looked at her again. "Dorothy, Look well. I'll never need another daughter in my family. Tell me, Dorothy, who is going to promote my name?" He shouted with tears in his eyes, "I am nobody."

Enoch rushed out, abandoning Rebecca and the baby. Rebecca was speechless as Enoch said good-bye to her.

One of the neighbors watched and shouted at him, "The community respects Rebecca! She doesn't need your money! The baby will grow up to be a fine, beautiful woman. Enoch, you will regret your attitude and whatever you have said, to your grave."

His persistence in denying the baby moved the two women into action.

They jumped up and ran to him. They said, "Man, you are never to dictate the gift from God." Then they ran after him, saying, "You can't choose, you can't choose."

On the seventh day after the baby's arrival, a group of women held a naming ceremony party for the baby. Josh Dele, Enoch's relative, named her Helen.

As the years passed, Helen got a reputation in the little Christian town along the River Niger as a restless, crying little girl.

As Helen sat outside the door crying, Josh watched her, then he said, "Helen wants the attention and love that she never received from Enoch when she was a baby."

Dorothy laughed and walked over to Helen. "Helen, you're a special girl. You're very beautiful. We love you." She hugged Helen and kissed her cheek.

Helen ran inside the house, smiling, waiting for her father.

One day when Helen was three years old, Rebecca thought it was a peaceful morning, and the day was bright and sunny, as she left Helen in the care of seven year old Judy, then dashed to her father's house, which was a few blocks away.

A few minutes later, Linda Jordan, Rebecca's best friend, came in and asked Judy, "Where is your Mama?"

Judy said, "Sorry, you just missed her. She went to see granddaddy."

Helen backed away from Linda and started screaming.

Linda said, "Don't sass me, little wise girl Helen. Judy, go and call Rebecca. Tell her I'm waiting."

Judy agreed and ran with enthusiasm.

Helen looked and said, "No, no, don't touch or hold me, Linda. You are a bad woman."

"Linda asked, "Helen, how do you know?

Helen replied, "Because you do bad things, and you want to do harm to my mother, Rebecca."

Linda looked at Helen and said, "Don't talk to me like that, little girl, or this time you will have it."

Helen screamed and said, "I can see you, bad woman."

Linda opened Helen's mouth and ordered, "Little girl, open your mouth."

Helen got up, but Linda pressed her down and forced her mouth open. She poured liquid into her mouth and quickly ran away.

Helen was alone, and she started crying.

As Rebecca headed home, she heard Helen crying. Helen then cried out, "My father, Enoch, they're hurting me. A woman is hurting me."

Rebecca entered, looked at her, and asked, "Where is Judy?"

Rebecca ran out and cried, "Help, help me. Helen is in trouble. Please help Helen." She felt like her world had exploded, then she panicked.

Goodman Henry a native doctor, rushed in, and said, "Rebecca, don't cry. Helen will be fine."

Many people ran from all over to help. They said, "Helen must not die. Who wants to harm little Helen?"

Fear spread all through Rebecca, and her heart ached. She looked at Helen and said, "Only God could handle every family crisis." She held Helen, knelt down, then folded her hands in prayer.

The people around prayed with her. Goodman gave Helen native leaves mixed with water to drink. Three hours later, she regained her strength.

Rebecca became very sad and afraid, watching over Helen. The distant love echoing in her for little Helen made her more anxious and frightened for Helen's future. She is pregnant and hoping for a son.

A few months after Helen's third birthday, Rebecca gave birth to a baby boy named Benson. This time, Enoch held a party to celebrate his son's arrival.

Judy was beautifully dressed with beads of different colors that Enoch had bought her. The beads were wrapped around Judy's waist and made melodious sounds as she walked. This was a sign of good life and of a child Enoch loved.

It was fascinating as Judy walked nude with the beads around her waist. They made quick, clicking sounds, and Judy was proud and very happy. Judy's appearance showed the character and worth of Rebecca and Enoch in their community.

But Helen wasn't dressed in that manner to commend her beauty. Helen's natural beauty was her weapon. Helen watched Judy wearing the beads, and tried to remain cool and uninvolved. She said, "I shall make my own beauty, daddy."

Three months later, Enoch and his relatives walked into daddy's room with a woman. She became Enoch's second wife.

Five years later, Rebecca called, "Enoch, please come." Enoch came and sat down, looked at her and then asked, "What do you want?"

"You never talk about Helen. Helen is ready to start elementary school, Enoch." He got up and shouted at her, "No, no! Helen is not good for school."

"Why, my husband?" Rebecca countered.

He laughed and said, "Helen is only good for marriage." Rebecca did not say a word, but the next week, Rebecca took Helen and walked her the three miles to school.

One year later on a bright afternoon, Rebecca found some fruit in the living room. Because she loved to eat fruits and vegetables, she joyfully ate them. A few minutes later, Lisa Onik, Rebecca's sister, arrived. Rebecca asked, "Where have you been, Lisa?"

Lisa replied, "Sister, I'm just coming home." Rebecca looked and asked, "Who put the fruit in the living room for me?"

Lisa looked at Helen and said, "I wasn't home and we didn't receive fruit in school today."

Helen ran and hugged her mama.

Lisa said, "Maybe, sister, that bad woman Linda put the fruit here."

Rebecca rushed into her bedroom, frightened, sad and worried.

Three days later, she became very weak. At about midnight, her words made Helen's heart ache.

Helen knew it wasn't what Rebecca really wanted, but was tired and her body was a painful prison for her. The two sisters nodded that they understood. Helen squeezed her hand.

Rebecca smiled weakly and whispered, "Always stay together."

Helen and Judy cried for help, calling, "Mama, Mama!" Rebecca never answered and never woke up. She died in Helen and Judy's arms.

Linda's husband, Joseph, was Enoch's best friend. He too was at the funeral. He called out to Linda and asked, "My wife, Linda, who did away with Rebecca?" Linda looked at him and did not say a word.

Joseph was angry. He asked again and again, "Tell me, Linda, who killed her, wicked woman?"

Linda said, "I can't tell. I'm very sorry. If you ask me more questions, you won't live long either." He gazed at her, frightened.

"I'm very sorry, Rebecca," said Joseph. "Some of us can't understand what brought about your sudden death. Let your soul rest in peace. Helen will survive," Joseph cried.

Linda called out to Helen and Judy said, "Why is Linda looking at us? She is a bad woman. Helen, don't go." Judy then repeated. "She is a bad woman."

Helen went to Linda and Linda said, "Oh Helen, your love never saved your dear mother. Your father never loved you because you were born a woman." Linda turned her face and started walking away.

Helen watched Linda as she walked away. "I'm too young to fight you, Linda. You're right, I have no father who will listen."

A half an hour after the burial, Helen said, "Look, Judy, Daddy is walking briskly back from fishing. He never even attended the funeral. What type of man is he?"

Judy said, "I can't believe my eyes. It is true, Daddy is happy that Mama is dead. Is he happy?" Judy asked again and again. Helen and Judy cried louder, looking at Enoch.

Helen said, "Don't worry, Daddy. Mama is gone with her wealth. Tomorrow is another day." The two sisters cried, "Mama is dead. We are her image. Mama's name will never die as long as we live."

After three years, Enoch became depressed. He felt lonely, unsatisfied, and disappointed with his life. He was sad and poor, crying all day and night, calling for Rebecca who was long dead. The birth of Benson never brought happiness to Enoch. He felt and always said, "Rebecca, you were my true love."

Helen and Judy began to feed him. One day, they saw him come back from fishing with an empty net. They ran to him and laughed, then asked, "How many fish did you catch?" They ran in circles around him, laughing. Enoch sorrowfully entered his living room. He looked at Judy as she touched her waist.

Helen watched and wondered after Rebecca's death.

She never understood what happened to Judy's beads. One day she said, "Judy, let's sell your beads." Judy picked up her books and left the room quickly to join her friends.

A few minutes later, Judy came back. She looked at Helen and buried her face in her long hair, crying. Judy never explained. She desperately tried not to reveal her dad's behavior because she was Daddy's little girl. She shouted, "Helen, leave me alone," then ran back to her friends.

Helen stood and envisioned the happy life she had with her mother, then she ran and shouted, "Oh, we must work hard like our parents, motherless like them."

Chapter Two

Helen and Judy lived a good life when Rebecca was alive, but, though they were happy, there was something wrong.

Enoch Brown often beat his wife Rebecca and shouted at her. This was so because Rebecca had more money than Enoch. She wore nice expensive clothes and ate better than Enoch after his second marriage.

During Enoch's marriage to Rebecca, he was a heavy drinker. After drinking, he became violent and talked abusively.

Rebecca would take Helen and her son Benson, and secretly run to her father's living room. She only returned when Judy called, "Daddy is sleeping." She never fought with Enoch.

Enoch was very thin because of lot of heavy alcohol consumption, and his meals contained a lot of fish and meat. His excessive drinking never led to cirrhosis of the liver, but he lost his wife and his self-respect. He talked, but nobody listened.

Before Rebecca's death, one Sunday evening Rebecca had said, "Helen, let us visit granddad." They sat in granddaddy's living room and Rebecca said, "Helen, it's time to teach you about men and life." Helen was nine years old.

"I beg your pardon," Helen said calmly.

"I never wanted Enoch Brown," Rebecca continued. "My father forced me to marry him."

Helen said, "I have no idea what you're talking about."

Rebecca replied, "Helen, you will know and understand when the time comes. Be very careful to select your husband. Never rush into marriage." Helen listened.

Enoch Brown was a sad, failing man after Rebecca's death because the progress and fame of the family died with her, as well as Enoch's name and status. Helen and Judy worked very hard collecting walnuts to feed themselves.

Two years later, Helen said, "Enoch, our Mama is dead, and we can't feed you so go to your lazy wife. No more food." Helen slammed the door, and again, she said, "We're not your wives. Mama is gone. Are you happy now? Remember, you never buried Mama."

Enoch was stunned and stood looking at Helen. Helen continued, "This is a nightmare, but it is also the reality. We're ready to work hard like Mama. The rich farmlands Mama inherited from her father could support us. Daddy, you will live to see us proper in your lifetime." Helen slammed the door again. "You never even visit our farms." She cried, "Mama is gone!"

After Enoch returned shamefully to his wife, Helen went to her stepmother. She said, "Feed your husband. He does nothing for us. We can't feed him for you. Do you hear me? Feed your husband."

Chapter Three

Helen spent a lot of time making friends and playmates, mostly on Sundays. These friends loved Helen and stayed by her side when boys tried to beat her. Helen was popular among her mates, but her life was empty without her mother.

Helen didn't know then that the kind playmates could create a stronghold for her. She acted, behaved, thought, produced and delivered like a man.

One bright, sunny and hot afternoon, while Helen was on her way home from school, three fabulous muscled wide-shouldered boys her age staged a war. She was beyond speech. She yelled for help, but realized her friends were long gone.

The boys reached for her, pushed and kicked her, and tried to tear off her clothes.

Helen looked around, but there was no one to help. She shouted, "Today, you will know I'm not just a woman." She kicked them back with all her strength, then fell and crawled away.

They looked at her, and screamed, "Who are you, woman."

On their knees, they said, "Sorry Helen." Then they ran away.

Helen and Judy knew it wasn't right for Enoch not to support them. Helen started to lose her senses because the two most important people in her life had deserted her. Helen felt more lonely than she had at any time in her life, so she went to her mother's grave and prayed. Then she broke out in the cold sweat when she recognized and heard unfamiliar voice.

That was when Helen began to hear a voice in her mind, a message that described a perfect man who could adore her. The voice said he would never ask her to be anybody she wasn't willing to be. He was ready to wait and would spend his lifetime with her.

He was a tall, handsome man. All the parental love, all the boyfriends Helen had never had, was all wrapped up in one unbelievable package. He would be very loving and supportive.

Helen made it through the twelfth grade without letting this man's feelings bother her. She kept all the hurt to herself, hoping that through hard work and the knowledge of Christ, all would be fine.

Helen spent most of her time protecting other people with troubled-heart feelings. This character trait was formed in Helen's early childhood so that she would be the perfect wife, mother, protector and healer.

Helen saw all human beings as brothers and sisters. Her helplessness made her more reluctant to accept men into her life because men tried to control her life. She never trusted them.

When Helen's trust was betrayed, her feelings reflected the loss of her mother, who was the only person who had loved her. Her social life was then immediately affected, as Helen would withdraw to a little corner.

Being born a woman, and Rebecca's death, hurt Helen's social and love life and made it a vacuum. She felt like a failure, ashamed, lonely and hurt. She felt good things were far away from happening. But the worst was seeing her friends who had mothers.

She couldn't forget the year 1955, when Rachel Anthony's mother said, "Helen, you can't follow Rachel home."

"Why, Mary?" asked Helen.

Mary answered, "Because Rachel's suitor is waiting. And you, Rachel, beware of your beautiful friend talking to your boyfriend."

Helen looked and moved three steps. Then turned and said, "Mary Anthony, I'm aware you're a matchmaker. As for me, I have goals in life; I'm not hurting for married men. There's social changes on the way that will bring more women to educational institutions and well-paying jobs. Our generation's lives are dramatically changing for the better. The idea that women are only good for marriage and men will soon become an old tradition.

"Rachel's man is married, Mary," Helen continued. "Michael Dolly was married in church. He can't divorce his wife. Rachel is a mistress."

Mary said, "Helen, I wish you could give yourself a little time."

"A little time for what, Mary?" asked Helen.

But Mary was afraid to talk. She finally said, "Let me be honest, Helen."

"What are you trying to say, Mary?" Helen asked.

Mary answered, "Don't worry about what the man will think."

"Think what?" asked Helen.

Mary looked at Helen and said, "Think you're not being good and nice if you are his mistress.

"Remember, Rachel, I'm your mother. What you think of him and how Michael treats you count. No man worth your time will continue to treat you in a way that makes you uncomfortable."

Helen faced her friend Rachel and said, "Believe me, your mother, Mary, is pushing you into a love many experts warn against. Michael Dolly tries to manipulate women. He advances, then retreats, faking apologies to rekindle their trust and love. Michael is not in love, Mary, with Rachel.

"My friend," said Helen, "you have heard us. Rachel, you can't be like Mary. We must take responsibility. We must use the little opportunities we have to make life better for us. Then life may be better for our daughters than it is for us. That's my advice, Mary," Helen went on. "You're too lazy. Work hard to support your children."

Six months later, Rachel's love affair with the elementary school headmaster was still going on. Michael was thirty years older than Rachel, but their love continued, burning like fire. While school was in session, they would meet. It wasn't a silent affair any longer. Helen was in the middle, battling for her best friend.

The romantic farce moved the eleventh-grade pupils to action, and Helen finally said, "Rachel, we can't stand to see you so deep in love with that womanizer. We are going to report him. We mean your lover, Michael Dolly. What the two of you are doing is not normal."

"Who says what is normal?" asked Rachel.

Tina Miller said, "Listen, Rachel, our friends and mates who are married join with their husbands. They are having legitimate sexual desires, love and enjoyment. Michael's fake love is wrong, Rachel. You must be ashamed of yourself. You're lying to yourself that he's going to marry you. Your ongoing affair is unethical. Michael must go."

Then the class of forty pupils started singing, "Michael must go, Michael must go," beating their desks.

A friend said, "That's Rachel's choice."

Tina said, "Friend, you're Rachel's role model. Get out of our sight. You will suffer with your baby."

Rachel and her friend ran away to protect their own self-esteem.

Helen said, "In a culture that fails to respect female sexual experiences, Rachel and her friend cannot be real women. They're just bad role models. And Mary is a bad mother."

Trying to act like a woman changed Rachel's life forever. She remained at home for seven school days. On Monday morning, Helen held Rachel's hand and dragged her to school.

Three months later, Michael requested a transfer and reunited with his wife. He never returned to say good-bye to Rachel.

Rachel lost her smile and her wonderful expected life with Michael. She lost her dreams, the power of being a headmaster's wife. Feeling like a princess, eating delicious meals, all these ending with fear and shame.

Helen said, "Rachel, kick him out of your system and life. Be comfortable. Shake off the shame and dash to school, like the old days." Rachel dashed to school.

Two years later, Rachel married an accountant and dropped out of school.

Now and then, Rachel would take Helen out after classes. One day, Rachel asked, "Helen, why are you so antisocial? No one ever gets past the wall you build around yourself, especially men."

Three days later, Helen was able to relate part of her story to Rachel. Helen said, "I have nobody. I'm alone in this world. I must not behave like you, whose mother is alive."

Rachel was sad. She asked, "What of your sister and your rich relatives?"

Helen looked at Rachel, then said, "They all want me to marry."

"Marry?" asked Rachel. "Even your sister?"

"Yes, even Judy," Helen answered. Then Rachel left Helen alone. Helen became even more lonely and afraid.

Helen planned the next road to take. She had no supporter, so she said, I'm sixteen years old, and I'm not in a hurry. I must wait for the man in my vision." She added,"Talk to me again. You're my comforter. Speak to me, small voice. I'm at your service."

Helen pretended to enjoy being alone. No one knew and no one cared that she didn't. Helen felt like she was dying inside. But the memory of a tall quiet man's dark eyes and solemn face had been a powerful source of encouragement. It was impossible to ignore the voice.

In December of 1956, Enoch wanted Helen to marry a young man who came home for Christmas, looking for a wife. Helen rejected and ignored her need to be helped.

Enoch said, "Helen, open your eyes and ears. Helen hear me out. Never, never should a beautiful girl be well educated. The role of a beautiful woman is to marry and have children." He never stopped talking and trying to marry Helen off.

He continued, "A beautiful woman doesn't need education. You're not good for school, Helen. A second daughter worth nothing, a woman worth nothing."

Helen laughed, while watching Enoch. She said, "Never tease me, daddy. There'll be other men, times and other days."

She came closer to him and said, "I'm somebody daddy. Is that why you abandoned me when I was born? Answer me, daddy. You won't have to worry about me. I certainly appreciate all your efforts, but know that I have many more years to promote your name. Where do you want me to start? Tell me, do you want me to leave?"

Enoch never said a word but looked at her with his head down and went away. Helen ran to him and said, "Wait, daddy."

She looked at him, then said, "Daddy leave me alone. Bringing me into this world never gave you the right to give me away so young in marriage.

"I'm just sixteen years old. I might be wiser than sixteen years old, but the years count, daddy." Helen continued, "I will marry my choice when the time is right."

Then Enoch chose to work on Judy, and Helen went to live with her Uncle and his two sons who were not ready to study and could not even wash dishes.

Helen worked very hard, like a slave, while the sons lived like masters of the home. They commanded Helen to prepare food and wash their clothes. She cooked and served eleven people before running to school.

One morning, Helen was already twenty minutes late to school. So she decided to take the bush shortcut. On her way into the bush, three men followed her. She ran and they ran after her. Helen was a very fast runner. She shouted, "Murderers, leave me alone. Help, help me!"

A few yards to town, the men stopped. They called, "Girl," and said, "never take this road to school. Next time, your luck will run out."

Helen, breathing very fast, afraid and crying, said, "Lord, thank you for saving my life."

Six months later, Helen said, "Although I suffer like a slave, this is better than marriage. Marriage is an everlasting prison of making babies." Helen's uncle and sons laughed.

One year later, Enoch returned with a new plan to marry Helen off. A young high school teacher, James Jeffry, had given Enoch $500 to convince Helen to marry him. With confidence, Enoch took the money.

Enoch looked at him and said, "Don't worry. I'm her father. This time she must marry you. Never be afraid, Jeffry," said Enoch. "Helen is yours. Be glad."

Jeffry said, "Helen is mine. Helen is mine. Are you sure she will accept me?" Enoch said, "Don't worry, son-in-law." Jeffry went joyfully boasting and told his friends about beautiful Helen.

One of Jeffry's friends said, "Do you mean Helen Enoch? Oh boy, she will never go for you, Jeffry. Helen is never ready for marriage. She is too good for you. Trust me," the friend went on. "Go and collect your money back. You're not Helen's type."

Jeffry looked sad and weary. Tears ran from his eyes like rain. Without hope, he left.

Three months later, Rachel sent for Helen. As they sat eating dinner, Rachel looked at Helen, then she said, "Mrs. Jeffry, soon your dreams and nightmares will end. You will be like us."

Helen asked, "Who is Mrs. Jeffry? Are you dreaming?"

Rachel looked at Helen and said, "This is my confession. Love can't happen unless you're ready to commit yourself."

Helen asked, "Who is talking about a troubled marriage? You know I don't want to marry at all yet. I'm not ready to discuss marriage matters, my dear friend. I know exactly what I want to do with my life."

Rachel asked, "Can you value a loving relationship between you and a man now?"

Helen said, "Tell me what is going on here, Rachel."

Rachel said, "Please be cool. Don't fight with me, best friend. This time it's for real. Your father, sister, and other relatives already gave your hand in marriage to Jeffry. You can't run any longer. I thought creating a love partner might be the ideal Christmas gift. You're the untouchable Helen. Love never breaks into your system."

Helen didn't say a word. She went back to her uncle and waited for her father, Enoch, to break the engagement news.

Chapter Four

One year later, when Helen saw Jeffry, she threw the money at him. Helen said, "Jeffry, listen. Enoch always wanted me to be a man. He can't have it both ways. You can't buy my love."

She looked back and said, "I'm free. Love is a process that needs hard work and courage. You can't buy my love. I'm buying a better life for my future children. My dream of freedom from a false marriage will become reality."

Jeffry marched to Enoch and shouted, "Helen has bought her freedom. I couldn't bear to leave my money for you because you can't force her to marry me. She is too tough. Helen controls her life, not you, Enoch. I certainly appreciate your desire for me to be your son-in-law, but all is over." Jeffry readily agreed and disappeared outside leaving Enoch in the shadow of thoughts.

When Helen's freedom was restored, her spirit woke up and she began to hear the voice again. She listened and said, "That is fine. I must wait for the right time."

One bright Sunday afternoon, Helen looked through the window and saw a man with a big hat. She ran out and looked closer, then she ran and hugged Enoch. Enoch looked at Helen and laughed.

Enoch said, "Be happy, Helen."

"What's the news, Daddy?" Helen asked.

"Results are out," he replied.

Helen ran to her room and started praying. Enoch entered and said, "Helen, your result is one of the best in your school. You did very well." She laughed and hugged Enoch again and again, then she drank a small glass of red wine.

In her mind Helen said, "Daddy, I'm one step ahead of your plans." Four weeks later, she was called into the teaching service and Helen became an elementary school teacher.

One Sunday afternoon, Eric Bernard visited his friend Paul, Eric looked and saw a beautiful face coming his way. He looked again and thought how nothing would please him more than to see a relationship develop between them.

A few minutes later, he walked towards Helen until their eyes met. They looked again and laughed. Eric had a gentle smile and he touched her hand.

Helen groaned once, silently. She wouldn't let him know that she might like him, too. His eyes narrowed, his lips pursed as he watched her small body coming to life like a baby coming out of deep sleep. They talked and laughed for half an hour.

When Helen met Eric Bernard, she thought her dream had come true. It was so because Eric wanted a well-educated woman. Eric wanted a partner, not dead wood in the home. He was ready to wait for Helen.

Helen walked with Eric, trying to make a smooth, genuine transition. She couldn't help coming on strong as usual. This time Eric tried to be quiet. He seemed to enjoy her jokes and flattery. He looked at her and laughed.

Eric was a fantasy lover. He was what Helen's mother

would have called a well-loving young man. He cared for a better future. Eric was thin, and not much taller than Helen's 5'7", he had fine manners and was very brilliant.

He said, "Helen, I'm interested in you and your attitude about life. Your reasoning and behavior are more mannish, not feminine. Feminine women are always ready to chop and chop. They also want many children for cultural status and money. Such women never understand that many children need lots of love and parental responsibility."

Eric's soft voice, sweet smile and dedication to his education melted Helen's icy heart. She felt relaxed talking to Eric, almost girlish, a new feeling for her.

Eric watched, looked, and smiled, then said, "I wish you were ready, Helen."

Paul Parker joined Eric and Helen. Their lunch dates progressed to dinner after a lot of running around in the evening, and from then on, it was easy for Eric and Paul to know Helen better.

Eric said, "Paul, Helen is not our sexual symbol. She is a friend of equal status, belief, hope and worth. She is educated."

The image of a man the voice told her about grew clearer and stronger. This time Helen was happier and free from fear. Eric felt he was passionately in love.

Helen asked, "Am I a real woman?"

Eric and Paul laughed.

Helen tried very hard to ease off from her usual domineering self. She strained and toned down her voice. Then Helen cut back on her sports too. She only played basketball when Eric was around.

A few weeks later, Eric and Paul joked, "Helen, are you a man or a woman? Who are you?" For Helen still acted more like a man, although she dressed feminine.

Eric and Paul didn't really notice Helen's role-playing because Helen was pressuring them to recognize her as an equal, not as a woman. She sensed it was really her beauty that drew them closer.

Three months later, for the first time, Helen felt the way a young girl feels when she is being courted. Eric said, "Never doubt, old habits die hard and almost always return." Helen knew she wasn't drinking like men or talking loud like men. She didn't *love* men like men love women. It was just an exciting time for her. "Is this real?" Helen asked. She didn't realize she was slowly reverting to a woman's character, and she became more and more beautiful. She fit close to Eric.

Eric handled Helen's confusion with his usual calm and good sense by saying, "Take your time. I'm with you. Never run away from me."

A change of heart came over Helen. She was very self-conscious. Helen never thought the change in her heart would ruin her relationship with Eric and Paul.

Eric said quietly and carefully, "It's not that simple. Please don't go on like this, Helen."

Helen gazed at Eric, then she said, "I have made up my mind. I need space, that is all. I love you, Eric, but I can't live like this anymore."

He replied, "What do you want, Helen?"

Helen continued. "Eric, if you can't change, it has to be another man."

Eric asked, "Who is that man?" "Is he better than me?"

She screamed out of control, "You have found a lover, haven't you?"

Helen looked and said, "You might say there is another man in my life, too."

"Am I wrong?" Eric asked.

Helen said, "The other man is the one talking. I don't know where he has gone. I miss his tender touch."

Eric shouted, "What are you talking about, tender touch?"

"Your tender touch, Eric," Helen replied.

Eric laughed, he said, "You are crazy, Helen."

Helen began to pace back and forth, crying and waving her hands, then she said, "Eric, I don't expect you to understand."

"I need someone softer, I guess," Eric reasoned. "You have so much anger bottled up inside you. And you won't talk about it. I can give you what you need, but I can't go on getting nothing from you."

Helen asked, "Are you saying, I need some kind of creep to go digging around in my head? There is nothing wrong with me, Eric."

He took her to a hotel and rented a room. Drinks and food were served, then Eric said, "Feel at home, my love." They ate and laughed.

Eric started to touch her and she began screaming like one of the peacocks at the farm. Helen didn't stop herself, even though she was probably driving him off all the faster.

She hurried into the bathroom to hide from Eric. Helen thought later, it would be better if he had looked at her as a man. Eric couldn't understand or believe how a young, beautiful woman could never see herself as a woman.

Eric didn't know what to do. He added, "I will be in touch, Helen." Before Eric left he said, "Please Helen, if you want me, I will be around. Could you do me a favor and get counseling before you destroy yourself?

"Nothing is wrong with me, Eric," Helen countered.

"My father said beautiful women never make it through school. I promised Enoch then said "I will be the first woman in his family to be well educated. I shall be the good seed planted in the fertile land. I shall grow and bear fruit for people to eat. You will see me in your lifetime, and what my education can buy for me."

Eric was shocked and weary. He was speechless.

Helen continued. "You say I never made you feel alive. I'm not like the other women. I am who I am."

Eric swallowed hard and held his breath. He thought, "Maybe she has changed her mind."

Helen whispered in a small voice, "Eric, until you stop winding yourself into some kind of tight knot, I won't know what you want."

Eric never stopped trying. He said, "Nobody understands you, Helen. Your desires are far away. But try to understand my desires."

"No more talk, I need some space," said Helen.

He gazed at Helen and asked, "Are you telling me you never want me in your life anymore?" And with that little pause, his face screwed up. Eric's eyes were red as he watched her.

Helen was dismayed. She said, "Eric, you will always be a part of my life. But I will never allow you to ruin that part that is still me. I'm going to hang onto that. I will be in touch when I can work things out," she finished.

Eric was speechless and stunned. "She never sounded so determined before, he thought.

The voice said, "There's a good job to do, Helen." She put out her hand, and with pity, tried to wipe the tears from his face.

The voice said again, "Not yet." She gazed at him and said, "Eric, your desire can't be met now. You can do whatever you want with anyone. When you're free, you can come back to your roots. Maybe there might be a chance for us then. I have a job to do now."

Eric looked at her and said, "I love you very dearly, Helen," then he left.

Helen sank into a chair, worn out, feeling empty and helpless. She said, "Oh, Mama, I have done it again. I have driven away someone I called a friend. For a little while, he made me feel special and wanted. But now he's gone."

She felt betrayed and worthless again. I need love, she thought. Not just loved ones, but tender, gentle love, feelings and action.

Helen thought, "I'm Helen. If he loved me, he would learn to wait."

But inside Helen there was happiness. The voice said again, "I'm not in a hurry. He will be back when the time is right."

Helen went to her room. She remembered when Eric

said, "Get help before it's too late." Helen said to herself, "It's never too late, man. I have a job to do. You can enjoy yourself."

Two weeks later, Eric came back and said, "Little innocent Helen, you claim to never understand me, but you will understand this plan, Helen. I'm going back to school. I love you. One day, you will be mine." And then Eric was gone.

Helen's real-life nightmare started afterward. One man after another wanted to marry her, and were ready for marriage and children, but she hid out with Rachel, her best friend, then Helen managed to stop herself from hiding, and she said,

"Sister Judy, the stranger's face appears to me over and over again. I can't keep myself from trembling. No matter how hard I try, I can't get my mind off the face I see in my mind's mirror."

One Saturday afternoon, Eric stopped in and said, "Woman, if I can't have you, they will never have you either. I'm not as far away from you as you think. Honestly, soon they will all get into their holes where they belong. Take your time Helen, I'm not in a hurry." Eric dashed away.

"Judy," said Helen, "I can't forget his look. When I walked in today and saw Eric, the face in the mirror appeared again. Judy never opened her mouth.

Helen told Judy that she loved the face and felt herself unwinding right away. Helen laughed, still feeling good and fine. Still, Judy never said a word.

Three weeks later, Helen was told that Eric had fought with one of her suitors. The voice said, "Don't blame Eric. That suitor is sleeping with your cousin. He can't have you, Helen.

"Know this, you will never be any man's apparatus," the voice continued. You can't be used and adjusted to fit the message. You came to Earth for a purpose."

Everyone in the family was dancing to the tune of rich

and famous men. But Helen was holding out for equal partnership. She could only pray her strength would pull her through the roughest times ahead. Helen felt as though her life were falling apart. She said, "It's time to know the man the voice is talking about."

One Sunday afternoon, Eric and Helen sat in a classroom talking, and Eric said, "Helen, we need to know each other better."

She watched Eric and said, "I can't understand how the simple act of one small voice talking to me could change my life."

Helen looked over to the door to her room. She saw a man hanging around, watching. Helen said, "That is a crazy man. Eric is very traditional. He didn't want to see me deep in love before asking my family for the engagement."

Eric's love was a big surprise to Helen's relatives. Judy said, "Helen is the most critical woman as far as men are concerned. Just when the family begins to like and make a decision on one of her suitors, Helen will discover him always wanting to get married and having children. She will even find out if he's a lonely man without friends. Helen says a lonely man without friends is never in her book of life."

Helen laughed and said, "Judy, it's true such men make life very miserable."

Judy looked at her and said, "Baby sister, for our father's love, choose one. Daddy will disown you if you never do."

Helen gazed at Judy and said, "You know, Judy, I can't believe I'm old enough to get married. Why not you, Judy? Tell me the man in your life." Judy never said a word.

Helen watched Judy, then said, "You're the oldest, yet not married. Why me, Judy? Why me? This is more than I can handle." Judy tried to walk away, but Helen called, "Judy, wait. I can't marry that old lonely lawyer. He would be watching me in his mirror. Judy, look, Eric is young and willing to wait for me. Also, he is not ready for many babies. He's more interested in my education. Believe it or not, he stands a better chance to make me happy. He's in love with me."

Judy stood still, and said, "Baby sister, suddenly all things are fine. Our plans for your life we talked about are true and very important. Yet Helen, you must choose now."

"Why now?" asked Helen.

Judy laughed and answered, "Your beauty is against you."

Helen gazed at Judy, then said, "My beauty is not a asset anymore."

Helen whispered to her aunt Lisa, then they both laughed.

They ignored Judy's motives and jealousy. Lisa said, "Wait for your time and turn, Judy. Helen is not for an old lonely man. Give Helen a chance to choose, Judy."

Helen's heart lurched in quick beats and she felt like falling. She said, "I have one supporter. Thanks, Lisa."

Lisa and Helen laughed and quickly left Judy. Judy wondered what her next step would be.

Chapter Five

The moment became clear in Helen's mind. She was aware that Judy would continue to try to hurt her, so she played the role of a mother while carving a much better life for herself. Helen sent Eric to Judy.

Helen said, "Judy, here are three men. They all are loving men. You can make your choice."

Judy's enthusiasm just bubbled out over Eric, who won the game. But instead of being happy for Helen, Judy didn't want to talk to Helen after that.

She never cooked, but sat down and waited for her food to be served. Helen cooked and served Judy.

Helen and Judy always dressed like twins, but man problems built a great wall between them. Marriage became an enemy in their lives.

Helen totally separated from her relatives while waiting for her dreams to come true.

Lisa said, "I like your choice, Helen. You're twenty years old. Accept him. Let a new life take control."

The voice said again, "It's time to say yes. He is the man you're waiting for. He would be your father, brother, mother, best friend and husband. Don't run away, Helen. Judy adores Eric, but lies to you."

Eric just felt good to be around Helen. He never had a bad word to say about anyone, even when he would have been justified in doing so.

Helen was happy to hear Eric say, "Helen, you're a real beauty. You could only make my wedding lovelier by being part of it. Then headed, "Everything would just be perfect if you could turn to my world. It is waiting. It is not a dream and not foggy, but full of love and joy."

Helen was stunned as she listened to Eric. He was honest and loving. "This can't be true," she said.

Eric reassured Helen again and again, saying, "I will be there. There's no way that you are going to marry without me. I will be your groom."

Nothing will keep me from being with you. We would make a loving family. Time is tight, but I am able to rearrange my schedule. I shall wait. Take your time, Helen," Eric added.

Helen replied, "It's important that you wait if you love me, Eric. It's helpful knowing I have you on my side."

He smiled and said, "I will do my best to be cool, waiting."

Helen still wasn't sure. It frightened her to hold Eric's life in her hands. "If I can't move on to the next stage of my life, he at least has the right to his life," she acknowledged. "Time will tell if we are meant to be in love."

Three weeks later, Eric dropped in on Helen's doorstep. She was scared and Eric said, "I can't wait for you to write anymore. I can't keep from seeing you. I shall and must spend every weekend with you. You must give me a final answer. This is the only way to know if you really love me.

Helen looked at him and said, "Don't worry, you can take care of me in your heart. Your love will register in my heart. My spirit will respond. In a twinkle of an eye, a good answer will be ready. Do not be afraid, Eric," she finished.

Eric was punished at school for staying away every weekend. He had to sweep the dining hall and wash dishes for two months.

Eric said, "My friends, I'm not worried, knowing Helen will be mine."

Four weeks later, Eric visited Helen, and it was not fun. Eric wanted an answer from Helen. He said, "Answer me, my love."

The voice said, "It is right to give Eric your answer. He will not leave you alone. He will not function well in school without you. He is in you as you're in him."

Helen still pretended to be naive. She said, "Eric, you are a wonderful man and I appreciate your being with me. Maybe there is a force behind this, our love. And maybe we are destined to be husband and wife. Do you feel what I feel, Eric? If you do, my answer is your wish."

"What, Helen? Say it again to my ears," Eric gasped.

Helen said, "I shall marry you."

"Are you sure, Helen?"

"Yes," replied Helen. "I cannot deny your love for me.""Listen, Eric, nobody can stop me from loving you. It's approved from the highest authority. Go back to school; I'm yours forever. Death may not even separate us. I'm ready. Take me to your world."

Eric laughed and sat down. He couldn't believe what he had heard. He asked, "Is that true? Do you promise?"

Eric faced Helen and sang, "Never make a promise in vain. Never make a promise you will never keep. Don't say you love me, if you can't keep your promise. Never make a promise you can't keep. But make me a promise you must keep." That was Eric's first song for Helen.

Helen felt joy in her heart, and she said, "It's not right to deny you my love. Eric, know the truth today. I do not have the power to keep my love from you anymore."

She cried herself to sleep with Eric's arms around her.

He watched her as she struggled to find relief from the pain of her decision. Each looking at the other's face was a challenge. It was a challenge for her because, yes is yes, No is no, and there was no turning back.

After Eric and Helen promised to love and cherish each other, her pain finally ended. Love took over and started growing. Nobody could convince Helen against Eric's love. She accepted the shocking truth that she adored Eric as much as he adored her. He put his head on her chest and wept.

She asked, "Can you wait, Eric?"

He said, "We are going to be great together. We are two lovers in one body." He kissed her and kissed her again. His kiss grew deeper and more probing.

His hand found its way, but Helen said, "Not yet to your underworld, darling Eric." Eric watched her face and smiled.

Helen's heart ached for him. She said, "You are an intelligent, capable man. You are so much more to me. There are so many men, good smart men out there who wouldn't wait. I'm sure we'd be great together. I'm sure we *will* be." They laughed together and smiled together.

Helen held Eric's hand. She looked and said, "Lord, create in me a more pure heart. A pure heart to love and obey you more, Lord. Create in me a pure heart to see the truth. And keep your spirit in me that I may love you more, Lord. For all the knees shall bow, and all the tongues shall shout Jesus! and all the knees shall bow, and all the tongues shall sing praises to the Lord. All tongues shall shout, Jesus you are the Lord. Create in me a pure heart to obey your command and see the truth of your glory. Yes, you are the true God our Father, the everlasting Father. Create in me the true light of God. Fill my empty life."

Chapter Six

Helen hurried to her mother's grave, still in a mixture of emotions. She fretted, fumed, and screamed of feeling helpless. She said, "How cruel life is. There is no Mama to help me make this decision."

Helen said, "Mama, I have started to love a man, but none of my relatives ever approved of him, I'm afraid, sad, and I cry every night. How can I tell whether you wouldn't disapprove, too?"

Helen screamed very loudly, "Talk to me, Mama." She began rocking back and forth. She started crying and calling, "Mama, hear my voice. Answer me, Mama, talk to me."

The voice never talked again for she already had made her choice. Eric was ready to change her quiet life. He would not turn a blind eye or look the other way.

Then the unbelievable happened. Eric immediately hurried to his friends, and said, "She promised never to turn back. She is mine. Helen is mine. We will make it together.

"She is mine, she is mine."

"Who gave her to you, Eric?" Paul asked.

"Just wait to see and hear her when she returns," answered Eric.

Helen was too young to know the toll Eric's love was taking. But one thing she had control over was whether or not to sleep with him. She always remembered and told herself, "I must not give myself to Eric yet. I must be ready for my goals and his plans for our future."

Eventually, Eric honestly couldn't wait any longer. Helen started doing many things to keep him out of her way, but she could not do all of them at the same time. She started counting her priorities more and more.

Eric then visited Judy and said, "In three days time, we are going to visit my father-in-law. We are going to buy my freedom. Yes, yes, my freedom."

Judy was sad and surprised, and she wondered why such an agreement had escaped her ears. She looked with a frown on her face.

Eric said, "Judy, your father does not want you to know, but I must tell you the truth. You can't stop our marriage anymore. Do you hear me, Judy?" asked Eric. "Your father said you're a jealous sister."

Enoch, his relatives, and the leaders of the town community jointly accepted his marriage proposal to Helen. They said, "Go in peace. Take Helen, she is your fiancee." From that day, Helen became Eric's fiancee, waiting for him to pay the dowry.

Judy asked, "Is that why he refused to discuss the matter with me? I visited him two days before he left town."

She became angry and shouted, "You're not free yet, Eric!"

Eric said , "Judy, you can't stop our marriage. Already, drinks and money have been received as part of the African marriage custom.

The next day, Judy hurried over to visit her uncle with the strange news, then later she said, "I'm the firstborn, I have my rights, Eric. You can't marry Helen. Wait to see the power I have in this family."

Helen went into her room, and showed three pieces of wrapper, headties and shoes to Judy.

"What have you done to me, Helen?" waited Judy.

Helen said, "Judy, you can't control me. You're my sister, not my mama. Eric is our choice my choice."

Eric kept laughing. "Be watchful. She could lie awake at night thinking and planning for the worst. You are an easy target, darling; you could be dead next."

Helen laughed and said, "Look at me, Eric. There is a greater power controlling all of us. She cannot change my destiny. Look at us. I'm different from her, so our destiny is different from hers."

Judy argued back, but Eric said, "After all, you never wanted Helen to marry a well-educated man. It is only so because you have not found a better lover yet."

Eric continued. "My darling Helen, your father is right. Everybody, even Judy's boyfriend, says she is jealous of you. You serve Judy, cook for her, honor her, and respect her. Is she a mother or a jealous sister?

"Time will tell said Helen "She has wanted me to marry since 1956."

"Why is Judy behaving this way?" asked Eric.

Maybe to avoid competition, Helen replied, "Little sister never competed with Judy before."

Eric looked at Helen and said, "You are too beautiful, Helen. There is nothing she can do now. You are mine. I hope she can understand her role as a sister someday."

In August of 1960, Eric, Paul and Helen visited Enoch. The River Niger and the lakes around it were angry with high tides, so the journey took five days.

Immediately on arrival, Helen saw many eyes watching, and she turned and smiled at them.

Anna, her uncle's wife, hurried over to welcome them. She said, "Come in and feel at home. My husband, your uncle, will soon return." Other relatives stood around watching.

Helen quickly followed Anna to the kitchen, and Anna said, "Eric seems okay." Helen and Anna laughed.

Judy mused over their attitude in the kitchen. A moment later, Helen joked, "A promise is a promise. I guess we shouldn't let them down." Judy looked at Helen.

Eric quickly started a loving song, and they finally settled down and cheered each other.

Paul sat close and became attached to Judy. They enjoyed the evening, dancing and drinking wine and beer. They felt so good together.

The following morning, Anna, Judy, Eric, Paul and Helen left to visit Enoch. A party was held after the dowry was paid by Eric.

Enoch was very happy and pleased. He prayed and blessed Eric, saying, "I love the courage you put up to stand for what you believe to be yours. That's the role of a real man, Eric. Helen is yours. Go and see her uncle to complete our cultural tradition."

After the dowry was paid, Helen was fully Eric's fiancee. He had all rights to have her and love her. Any man who sexually harassed her would pay a large sum of money to Eric's family as African traditional culture decreed, stage two of the code of marriage contract.

Helen summoned up her courage, put on her smiling face and walked to the door. With trembling hands, she opened the door, then she ran out and cried.

Once outside, she trembled with fear. Helen said, "Oh, my freedom is gone, Mama." Tears filled her eyes.

Nobody noticed Helen's cries. They all understood that she never wanted to marry so young, although, to them, twenty years of age was not young.

By the time Helen got back to Eric, he was playing with his food. Eric also shed tears of joy.

He said, "Come, darling, it is okay and fine now. Don't run from me. We are one."

"Are we?" asked Helen. She gazed at Judy and smiled.

A few minutes later, she settled down, looked at him, and said, "I'm fine. Nothing I could not handle, though it seems like a dream."

Helen seemed to wake from a second sleep with a strange feeling. She became more attached to Eric because he had understood what happened. Helen gazed at Eric and said, "I can't go with you feeling like this." She began to cry again.

Eric felt worried. He asked, "If Helen loves me, why do her cries never stop? Something must be wrong. We must leave now for her uncle's place." Helen felt relieved to hear Eric's voice.

Enoch answered without looking at Helen, "You know how women are, Eric. Helen is just happy."

He said, "Darling, be happy. You are finally mine. All I can say, is, this is the happiest day of my life."

The engagement party ended, and Eric and Helen took off, followed by Judy, Anna and Paul to her Uncle's village.

Chapter Seven

On the way, they encountered a heavy storm on both land and river, and the canoe started sinking. The ladies shouted, "Oh, Eric and Paul can't swim. What can we do?" Eric and Paul held the edge of the canoe, while the three ladies paddled the canoe as quickly as their energy could pull it.

The storm continued, turning and tossing the canoe. Anna started crying.

Judy said, "Sister Helen, tell me."

"Tell you what, Judy?" Helen asked.

"Tell us what to do," Judy cried out.

The wind and storm became worse with heavy waves.

Helen looked at Eric and Paul., then said, "Yes, sister Judy, they can't swim. They are like a whole potato dropped in water. There is only one thing we can do."

"What?" asked Anna.

Helen laughed.

Anna said, "Your fiance and his friend can't swim and you're laughing."

Helen asked, "Can anyone guess what I have in mind?"

"Tell us," said Eric. "We're waiting—we can't swim."

Helen looked at them again and laughed.

Anna said, "Helen, we're talking about two lives. Just tell us."

Helen replied, "I believe we can seek help."

Helen watched the heavy storm tossing the boat. She believed there must be help. Waiting and thinking of what to do, she asked herself where is my faith, then she believed they could seek help.

"What help?" asked Eric.

Helen answered, "We can ask God our Father to help save us. The Lord our Father has the greatest power to talk to the sea. Only one thing to do; that is, we must trust Him and have our faith in Him. He will not let us die because we're His children."

Helen prayed and they all started singing church songs. Fear vanished. A sense of joy entered and took control of their minds. Quickly they paddled the canoe, which never tossed again.

Arriving home, they praised the Lord for His care over them.

Judy touched Helen with a smile, then said, "Truly God is with you."

They sang and praised the Lord for His greatest love.

Looking pretty and beautiful was Helen's usual way of life. That evening, she dressed especially well with beads to celebrate the official engagement and the paid dowry according to the African tradition. From that day on, Helen recognized Eric's right to have her as his fiancee.

They sang love songs, danced and drank wine and beer. They also ate well-prepared fresh fish and roasted chicken.

Eric and Paul told most of the love stories.

Anna became very happy waiting for her husband's arrival. She was excited being with them.

Anna smiled and said, "There is a new world."

Helen said, laughing. "This is part of being educated."

Anna shouted, "Oh yes. Now I understand why you refused to marry your daddy's choice."

"Don't tell uncle, Anna," advised Helen. "This is what men and women do in college."

Anna looked at Helen.

Helen kissed Eric. then said, "Anna, this is part of making love. Don't tell." African culture never cared for kissing. These are modern times.

Anna replied, "Oh no, I will never tell your uncle." They all laughed.

The next day, Uncle Ekini arrived, and he watched Eric closely, then said, "I'm very sorry for keeping you waiting, Eric."

Eric said, "Helen is worth every minute spent. I'm at your service."

Helen remained silent, waiting to see and hear Ekini's comment. Helen's mind reflected on the competition between her and Judy.

Finally Helen said, "Having a competitive younger sister can damage a woman's self esteem, and may even interfere with her ability to establish other successful relationships. I hope this is not you, Judy.

"But remember, Judy, I'll always support you and help you out of your problems. I never see you as a failure. Remember our relationship before men came into our lives. Remember when you once wanted me to marry. early. Remember when you never wanted me to be well educated, but just to get married."

Judy started walking away.

Helen said, "Come here, sister. It is not unusual for a grown sister to want independence from a competitive older sister. This happens because of feeling angry, which is never the solution because you cut part of yourself out. If you cut me out, you will be lonely forever, Judy."

Judy didn't want to listen, so she asked, "What do you want, beautiful sister Helen? You have everything a woman needs. Leave me alone."

"If you never think about your actions, at least listen now."

Uncle Ekini said, "Judy, let's hear Helen. She might be right."

"Fine, Uncle," said Judy. "She wouldn't be wrong."

Helen said, "It's better if we make use of all our connections."

"What connections?" asked Ekini.

"The knowledge we have to create a better life for all of us," Helen answered.

"Being furious with what we haven't got can't change the situation. Anger and fury will fade away. A good supportive relationship is the solution. Stop being emotionally defensive. The goal is to meet life half way."

"Go on, Helen," said her uncle. "It seems you know and understand more than we think. We have missed a lot, being far away from you."

Eric said, "If you're close to her, you will love her more. She has more to offer than she can take."

Helen continued, "The remedy for being jealous and furious is to speak out. Face your feelings. Never deny and hide them—that will destroy other love relationships. Really confront the anger and the hurt. Find the best solution to bring happiness."

Judy asked, "What do you want me to do, pretty one? You must be aware that this is your life."

"Yes, Judy," agreed Helen. "This is my life, sister. It is not what you want me to be. I want you to love me enough not to do damage and harm behind my back. Let's direct and focus our lives in the present. We must forget past grievances. This can diffuse some of our anger and bad feelings and we can once again be one family and two sisters in control of our lives. Remember, women have no place in the family. We must change this notion in our culture by improving ourselves."

Paul, Anna and Uncle Ekini looked at Helen. They said, "Yes, we learned a lot today. Hopefully, Judy will be a changed human being and a more loving sister. We hope she can try. This is an eye-opener."

Uncle Ekini made a sign, then bent his head. The sound of the sign seemed to reverberate in Helen's ears with a tinge of finality.

The moment passed in silence, and Helen thought of screaming with madness. She gazed at Eric, then looked at her uncle and saw that his face was deadly serious.

Sitting down close to her uncle, Helen asked herself, "What can we do now? I feel a terrible sense of foreboding. I never married their choice. They talk only of money."

There was something wrong about the way her uncle tried to avoid her eyes. Helen's voice portrayed her feelings of uneasiness. She asked repeatedly, "What's wrong, Uncle? Can't you be happy for me?"

Judy waited eagerly to hear her uncle's feelings. She wanted to find out if Helen could be treated better, whether Helen's actions and suggestions could generally change the cultural bondage of women.

Helen said to herself, My bondage must end today.

Judy watched Helen and asked, "Are we free? Can we make our own choices? If Helen does it, the feminist movement is on the go. Could she have what society calls a successful marriage?"

Helen laughed.

Uncle Ekini watched Eric's eyes, his movements and his attitude toward Helen, then he said, "Helen is the family queen. Are you sure you are the right man?"

Eric rushed to her side and placed his arm around her. She withdrew his hand. Her face showed confusion and fear. Never had she expected this from her uncle, Helen thought.

She felt so lost and alone because she had truly believed that Eric and she would grow old together.

Helen said, "Uncle, you know that, for so long I have loved Eric quietly and earnestly. I can't love another man.

I'm sorry, Uncle." We have never been overcome by passion. There is nothing between us that I cannot tell you about. Hopefully, it will work out fine for us. He seems to be my destiny. You know this, Uncle."

Judy laughed and went away.

Helen turned toward Eric and Paul. She looked at them, then faced her uncle. With that, she felt her vision nearly blinded by her thoughts and tears. Quickly, she wiped the tears away.

Anna turned towards Helen, and said, "Wait, my husband is ready, Eric."

Eric faced him, waiting for the uncle to speak.

Finally Uncle Ekini spoke. He said, "I have been deceiving myself. She has been with me because no one had come into her life. No man has touched her heart with ultimate love. How can I blame Eric?"

Judy said, "Helen is everything that I am not. Something I could never hope to be. Helen is moving modern women into modern times. She is becoming the role model. Hopefully, she is already a role model."

"Look," said her uncle, "a full moon has witnessed their blossoming love this night."

Judy looked at Helen and said, "There was no moon to watch my sorrow,"

Helen fell to Judy's knees and wept.

Uncle Ekini said, "I discovered you're in love, Eric. May God's blessing be upon you and my dear loving Helen. From now on, your freedom to have Helen and hold her is resting on you. Take care and love her. She is the family queen."

Uncle took a bottle of white gin and poured it on their heads, calling the forefathers for blessings.

Suddenly, Judy felt betrayed and drained. She said, "Deep inside, I knew today that true love couldn't be destroyed. In Helen's case, it could not be forced. When shall I be free, too?" Judy started to cry and ran to her bedroom.

Tears again began to stream from Helen's eyes as well.

Judy said, "Look at her, so young and beautiful. Her beauty frightens me. It frightens me realizing what I had tried to accomplish. Who can prevent what has been planned and blessed? Who can prevent destiny?"

Judy looked into Helen's eyes, mirroring her own anguish. Judy's voice was shaking, when she said, "You are behaving like my senior, Helen. That's my truth."

Helen knelt down, and there was silence, then Helen said, You're my senior sister, Judy. I will never become your senior. It is time for you, Judy, to understand the truth.

"What truth?" asked Judy.

Helen faced Judy. and replied, "Judy, you're the cause of my long waiting to accept Eric's hand. I loved him even before we discovered ourselves."

Wake up, my sister. I shall forgive you for whatever you attempted to do to me. There are many changes in a human's life. Better wait for your chance and time. I'm ready to support you though I'm your younger sister."

Helen continued, "Open your eyes, Judy. Age never makes us wiser, but in the way we think, act, and see our society. Remember this view in life to guide yourself.

"Come from darkness, Sister, to see the light." Helen continued. "Allow true light in you. You can become whole. Never feel disappointed when my wishes are granted. Watch how you react to prevent future damage. The true voice is watching us always."

Eric and Paul laughed, then Eric said, "Paul, never step into Helen and Judy's lives. They are very close. They behave like twins though from today, they will never dress like twins anymore."

Helen and Judy cried again and again for breaking the bond between them.

Eric rocked Helen to sleep while Paul rocked Judy. Then Eric and Paul drank until 4:00 a.m.

When Helen woke up, she found them talking, and she called, "Darling, go to bed." She took his hand and led him to bed. Paul followed.

Helen went to bed, put out the lights, and prayed. "Lord, your voice is heard. My life and progress are in your hands. Help me through this stage of my life." Then she slept.

Chapter Eight

One month later, Enoch wrote, "My dear son Helen, I'm very sick. During fishing, a fly bit my left eye. Not long after, the eye was swollen. Now, I can't even see with the eye. Help me, my son."

Three days later, Helen brought Enoch home for treatment. Goodman came, sat down and had a drink. He said, "Helen go back to work. Don't worry about your father. He is under my care. He will be fine."

Helen waited.

Goodman went to the bush and came back with leaves and roots. He squeezed water from the leaves and put three drops into each eye. Enoch shouted, "This medication is hot like hot pepper."

Seven days later, Enoch started to see with his eye.

Helen said, "Daddy, I'm not your son, I'm your daughter, Helen. Benson is your son. Do you understand, Enoch?"

Enoch raised his head and looked at Helen. "You are my son."

Helen said, "No Daddy, I'm born a woman, not a man."

He laughed and said, "I can only relate to you as my son, so you are my son."

Helen left Enoch with his relatives and went back to her teaching station.

On her way, riding her bicycle, she said to herself, "Why is Daddy calling me his son? I'm born a woman, not Daddy's son."

Chapter Nine

While Eric enjoyed his freedom and the luck of having a beautiful, educated fiancee, Helen's life became frustrated. Her plans were not working. Many men hated Helen for choosing Eric to be her future husband.

Three months after the engagement party, Edward Kafred, Helen's boss, invited her to his house. He threatened to write a defamatory character reference to the education board. This would stop Helen from going to Mission College should she ever want to. Helen sat ten feet away from him.

Edward said, "Helen, take a mirror and look at yourself. You're now calling yourself Eric's fiancee. Do you think we care? I must have you before him."

She shouted, "Over my dead body! No man has the right to have me except Eric. He is my fiance. Open your ears and hear me. Only him, not you or any other man," vowed Helen.

Edward replied, "Helen, choose between your career, your job, and Eric."

Helen said, "Edward, you can be my boss. You can give me a bad reference. You can deprive me from going back to college, but there is one thing you cannot do."

Edward looked at her and asked, "What is that one thing?"

Helen said, "You cannot force me to make love to you."

He laughed and tried to hold her.

Helen shouted, "You're a devil! You're married, Edward! Making love with you is a sin! I will never commit such a sin. I must never be the agent of your sin of adultery. Adultery eats away the trust in marriage and kills the soul and love for each other!"

She ran out and quickly rushed to her room. She opened her door, looked back and said, "Edward, you're in trouble."

Stress increased, but self-pity could only hurt her. Helen turned to her memories. She became her own guide again.

Helen said, "There is no one to fight this war for me. Little did I know when I fought my education battle." Still, her boss's bad reference made her life much more difficult and frustrated.

Her dream of having a solid education one day drove her to an unknown land, a land where the majority spoke no English.

Helen was waiting for a taxi when a stranger's voice shouted, "Helen, Helen." A man started waving his hand on the other side of the road. She wouldn't listen or look. She ran up the street. The day was getting dark. She continued running for a taxi. A few minutes later, two men got out of a car. She didn't want anyone to see her. She couldn't trust anyone.

The man shouted, "Don't try to cross the road. Just wait." Helen noticed dynamic power in the call. She felt controlled by the voice. She didn't move again.

Finally, two young men came and said, "Helen."

She looked and asked, "Do I know you? Who are you?"

"Don't you recognize us?" they asked.

Helen asked, "Who are you, in this big city, stopping me?"

She started walking slowly as she watched them following her., then she took off and ran 300 yards. They followed her.

The man said, "Look at us and listen to this voice. It's very tough to solve math. Don't hate me, for I love you and respect hard work. Work harder. The answer is in your hands. That's your future."

"Oh! no, this can't be true," Helen said. She looked at them and said, "I hope I'm not dreaming, Sammy?"

"Yes, Helen. I'm Sammy Johnson, your student three years ago."

She hugged him and said, "You're a man now."

"Yes, Helen," said Sammy.

Helen laughed, then she asked, "How is your sister?

Sammy answered, "She is married with two children."

Helen wasn't frightened anymore, but was stunned and couldn't move.

She then spent two days with Sammy, and they partied and visited many places. Sammy said, "Helen, one good turn deserves another. Without you, your kindness to us, we couldn't have achieved so much in our lives. Please accept our little way of saying thank you."

Sammy continued, "Helen, you are a good teacher. You are a role model to our sisters and daughters. We trust, no man can turn you into his dark world." She entered a taxi and rode off, waving her hand.

She said, "Thank you, Lord. This is my reward for good work well done. Teachers are the role models."

Once she was home, Helen visited Sammy and his friend's parents. They said, "We trust you, Helen. That womanizer, Edward, can't drive you away. The community loves you. Do not be afraid. You are a role model to our daughters. Never give up."

Chapter Ten

Four weeks later, a letter arrived, and Helen was eager to know the contents. She opened it and read: "Your grades and evaluation section are fine. We are sorry, but we can't offer you a chance in our college.

"The recommendation letter from your education board is very destructive. Your boss, Edward, characteristically destroyed you. We advise you to seek admission in a private or government college or institution, not a mission college. We wish you luck. We cannot change the rules."

She was silent, then later remembered what she said to Edward. "You're in trouble." She called for Eric who was visiting a friend. On his arrival, Helen appeared full of anger and distress. Helen said, "Edward's revenge has peaked—no let up."

Eric shouted, "That is sexual harassment, Helen. Oh, sweet, Edward is in big trouble. From the beginning in mission teaching work, you have been industrious, undeviatingly honest and impartial in handling your duties. Edward dislikes me. I'm your fiance, Helen. He must reap what he sows."

Helen was very angry and sad. She went out and looked towards Edward's house., then said, "The custom and culture of Africa will be your greatest enemy. In the higher mission service, you have broken the rules, even your pension can't pay."

Helen was back to square one. She wasn't recovering very nicely. One day, she decided to change her line of study. She was admitted into nursing school, which gave her hope and opened the door into her future career.

What Helen did not know was the control Eric's love had on her. His love took control of her life.

Eric said, "Helen, going to nursing school is the road to divorcing me. You would be too good for the medical doctors. If you love me, please never leave me for nursing school."

The light of his love shone daily and more strongly in her life. She kept seeing his face in the mirror again. Helen never made it to nursing school.

Eric said, "Yes, yes, my love is in control. I won again." He taught her many ways of being in love. Eric's love grew deeper and deeper in her life.

Helen once again felt depressed, but this time her strong desire for education helped her be more patient.

Eric suggested that she return to government college to complete the four years of college. Eric said, "Darling, it takes only nine months. That could open the road to achieve your educational goals and Edward couldn't stop you."

Seven days later, one early morning, Eric and seven relatives marched to Edward's house. One of the men practically broke down his door.

Edward, still in bed when he heard the banging, said, "You'll never sleep whoever you are."

Another man said, "Edward, your ambition and desire are your downfall. There's a gentleman to see you."

He opened the door. He was uncomfortable and distressed. He said, "No warning, Eric? So Helen reported."

One of the men said, "There's no good morning. You know the custom. Helen is ours. It will be well for you to pay $20,000 now."

Edward said, "Give me three days."

Another man shouted at him, "You know Helen's uncle is your supervisor. We must bring you in."

Now he began considering his discipline because the regulations and treatment of this type of offense are specific.

Another man shouted again, "Pay now and remain on your job, or pay three days later and move back home."

Eric looked at him and said, "You will be fired, Edward."

Half an hour later, Edward's business friend came in and begged with the money in his hands. On his knees, he said, "Gentlemen, Edward was wrong. Please forgive him." He put the money on the table.

Edward started shaking, moving up and down with fear. The youngest man counted the money and gave it to the eldest. Edward's appearance changed. He knelt down and begged for forgiveness.

Helen came in and said, "Edward, my goodwill could be important to protect your job. Now you know."

"You're quite right," said Edward. "Good-bye."

She watched him shaking his head with an angry face, then she whispered, "Good-bye, the future will tell," as she wondered what wrongs sexual ambition and harassment could bring on mankind.

Chapter Eleven

Once again, Helen kicked against her relatives, Judy and Enoch, who refused to support her education.

After eight years of teaching in the elementary school, Helen became a student. Judy rejected her, saying "Helen, take care of the training and feeding of a brother and a sister who are living with you. The family still sees you as a teacher." Right then, Helen felt more of a failure than she ever had felt before.

Helen asked, "Why are you doing this to me, Sister?"

Judy looked at her and laughed. Judy answered, "Can't you see why, beautiful one? You know you're more beautiful, more intelligent, and you have an intelligent, handsome man. The world is yours. You will be greater than I."

Helen said, "I helped to train you, Judy."

"Don't you know you're engaged?" asked Judy.

Helen turned her face and asked, "Judy, who trained you?" Her heart started racing forward. Never could she find words to match Judy's ill feelings and bad thoughts. Helen asked again, "Who trained you, wicked sister?"

Judy never said a word, so Helen said, "Remember, I'm not daddy's son."

With Eric's assurance, support, and love, she summoned up her courage, and dashed to school. No turning back.

Helen started having nightmares about whether she had made the right decision, then her relatives gave Eric a showdown. They called him a man without power. "Shame on you, Eric," they said. Eric was furious and felt ashamed.

He said, "Darling, move in with me and forget about going to college."

Helen kissed Eric lightly, then asked, "What kind of woman do you want me to be? You know I'm not like those women who love waiting for their husbands. I have a job to do. I must prove to my father he is wrong."

Eric grew annoyed. He took Helen's white bicycle and went to his teaching station. That never stopped Helen. She walked seven miles to school and seven miles to her farms with her brother Benson, who lived with her.

One Saturday afternoon, Helen thought back to the time, money and love she had wasted on Judy, Enoch and her family. She cried out, and wrote on her door: The downfall of a man is not the end of his life. The future will tell...

"God will answer my prayer to prove my worth," said Helen. "One day, Enoch, my daddy, will hug me."

Three days later, Eric arrived. He saw the writings, looked again and cried, too. Helen watched him and cried.

Helen said, "Those who suffer have the right to be happy. One day, my education will make me a happy woman and as good as a man."

A new feeling replaced Helen's anger. She was again attached to Eric, forgetting her stubbornness. Helen's dreams became more and more erotic and soon the dreams seemed very real to her.

Helen began to believe that Eric was actually her true love and husband. And whenever Helen looked at Eric, she thought about all the things her dreams had led them to do.

The hope for a better future depends on me working, thinking hard, and acting faster, Helen thought. Am I ready for this task? Will Eric appreciate it?

Eric was in honeymoon feelings when Helen heard her result. He hugged and hugged her for joy. Helen and Eric celebrated her success.

Eric said, "Helen, this is a big step. We're going to make it together." A big party was held for Helen's success.

Helen looked up to the white cloud, and said, "Mama, you would love to have witnessed this day and feel what I feel right now. Then you would have known, at first hand, that God loves us. You would have loved to have watched me work because then His greatest compassion and love for us would have been felt by all and Enoch.

Many men and women, including Judy, were ashamed. They recognized their foolishness, then continued to watch with interest what was going on in Helen's life.

"Another step forward will prove my worth," said Helen. "Daddy will see no difference between his sons and me. And, he will always find something good about having daughters like sons. Daddy, you are guilty of abandoning me! she cried.

Helen's promise before Edward and her community came true. Edward could not ignore the news. Helen's job was restored with an increase in salary.

This time, she had hope and courage. Her dreams were coming true, and she said, "The door of progress is opened. Thank you, Lord. Suddenly, everything will fall into place. Lord, your kindness will ever remain in my memory."

Helen became more quiet, silently watching those men who had higher degrees. She wished to share the pride and secrets of their achievement. She wasn't jealous, just a little sad that she wasn't more like them. It was because of job insecurity, not personal frustration.

Five years later, Eric's affairs caught up with him. While Helen was struggling to achieve her educational goals, Eric had been active, making babies with other women.

Women whose lifestyles and status depended upon the number of children they could have, hooked Eric. They never learned to read and write, but Eric had five babies with them.

Helen never cared about Eric's sexual affairs. She had nothing to do with women whose lives depended on moving from man to man. They made babies like chickens laying eggs. Eric was confused and ashamed, but he stayed with Helen, his fiancee.

One evening, when Eric visited Helen, he said, "When a man is sexually active and healthy, the body will talk. I need a sexually active woman, Helen."

She turned, looked at him, and said, "This is not a reason." She gasped. "This is pure unadulterated need. There is no denying that sparks fly between us, but I choose not to live my life waiting daily for sparks, without life goals. I know they can start a fire, but you have to remember that fires always burn out eventually."

Helen gazed at him. A wave of panic crossed from his face into his throat.

Eric suddenly realized he truly loved Helen, but his love was in trouble because of his affairs. "I love you, Helen," he said.

"Eric, I never cared about your affairs," Helen replied. "You call it an active sex life. I'm very sorry for you. One day soon, you will understand the silly mistakes you have made. You will be lonely and sorry, not just for losing me, but you will never be a good role model for your children. Sexual affairs are learned behavior. Your children are going to learn from their daddy."

Eric looked at Helen and said, "I'm not like you, who never cared about making love. I can't be like you, my darling. Do you understand? Men are all alike."

"I am giving you a reason, I shall stop you," said Helen.

His hands tightened on her shoulders as he leaned forward and swept his mouth across her lips.

Helen said, "Eric, sex has eaten your pride and worth. You are throwing your life away and we are drifting apart. There is no real love in your heart, Eric."

His manhood cooled down and Eric was ashamed. He said, "Please, Helen, understand."

"Understand what?" she asked and started to cry.

Eric shamefully said, "Basically, the reason I came no longer exists. No one has given me a reason not to leave." He stared at the truth hanging in the shadows of her eyes, accusing him.

"Those women will never replace you," Eric continued. I'm not ready to marry some illiterate. I wasn't even doing it for the babies. They trapped me."

"Don't cry," he begged as he scooped her up in his arms. "I didn't mean to make you cry." He feathered tiny kisses of repentance across her face.

"You never win, Eric, though you feel defeat is in my voice. Oh, no, they never forced you to make love to them Eric," Helen continued. "I wonder what type of a father you will prove to be. I poured my heart and love out to you, Eric. I'm not a sex mate, but a Christian."

She looked at Eric and said, "Just because they are not educated, you abandon four women and five babies! Please marry one of them and leave me alone."

"That can't happen," said Eric.

She looked up into his dark eyes, full of shadows and passion. The lights were still on. He shouted, "Oh, when I'm with you my lady, there is always light." Passionately, Eric began to touch her again and again.

After dinner, Helen sat Eric down, then said, "Respect is the foundation of any relationship, not just a marriage relationship or making babies. You know my principles. Eric, so go home. When you are ready, come to collect your dowry.

"Helen, give me a chance," he begged.

Helen continued, "You don't respect my feelings.

Whatever relationship we have is eventually going to fail. Eric, you can't make this marriage work because of your sexual activities. Go home." He left at 2:00 a.m. with a trembling heart.

Chapter Twelve

A week later, Helen was visiting a friend, when an elderly woman, about eighty years old called. "My daughter, come."

"I haven't seen that workman before," said Helen.

The old woman asked, "Why are you running away? You can't run away from your future husband."

"He is not my future husband anymore," said Helen.

The old woman looked at her and said, "Yes, he is. You can never, never run away from Eric."

"That's not true," said Helen. "He doesn't own me."

"He is your problem," said the old woman. "He will follow you wherever you go. Helen, you will never forget this day."

Helen talked to the old woman, who said, "Marriage is strengthened when couples learn from each other's differences and weaknesses."

"Not this type of difference," said Helen.

The old woman said, "You don't understand, little girl. You are here to solve Eric's problems."

"Not me, not me," said Helen. "I can't be his wife. I must accomplish my goals. Eric is not a part of my goals."

"The differences will make you stronger, and bring respect to Eric," said the old woman. "Eric can't accomplish anything good without you. Don't drive him away."

She looked at Helen and said, "The job is very hard, but there is nothing you can do to prevent your assignment. Know it from me today, Little Girl. You have carried this assignment since Eric was seven years old. You were one year old."

Helen said, "That's not possible." She walked out, came in again, and watched the old woman. Helen asked, "What are you talking about, Old Woman? How do you know this?"

The old woman said, "Your spirit protected him from the hands of those who read the book of life." Helen sat down and listened, unaware of the aim of the message.

Helen became terrified even more at her words. "They can't get him as long as you live. Your spirit does the job. You can't run away. Go and take up your job."

Helen began to cry. "I have no mother. My father never loved me. Nobody loves me. I can't be Eric's wife." She cried herself to sleep.

Three days later, Susan, Helen's mother-in-law, wrote Helen a letter: My dear girl, please forgive my son Eric. Please save him from all this mess. Please, for my sake, marry him. I love you from my heart.

Helen cried for three days. She was sad, depressed and stressful. She said, "My life is like a day when everything is wrong. I will never be a happy woman."

Helen's dreams, plans and the privilege would come with a high price and doubts about her ability to fulfill her role. "I can't perform impossible task because I'm a human being."

The wind was very warm and sweat dripped from her body. She went to the river to cool herself and swam for twenty minutes.

While Helen was lying on the sandbank of the river, Eric's sister, Darcy, suddenly called to her. Helen looked up, and Darcy came closer and hugged her. A few minutes later, Nark, Eric's brother, stopped by, too. Nark said, "Please Helen, we are here to set up a wedding date."

"With whom?" Helen asked.

Nark laughed, then said, "With Eric. There is no other way to stop his problems. You're the one, Helen."

Helen saw the tiny lines of exhaustion around their eyes. It was not pretense, but true love that would find a solution for Eric's problems. Helen looked at them, heavily troubled, then she asked, "Why me, Nark? Why should a motherless girl like me marry your brother, a womanizer?"

Helen asked, "Why is it my duty to break Eric's bad habits? How do you expect a woman who never loved another man to be enough for Eric? I have a little difficulty believing I'm the right woman for Eric."

"Yes you are," said Nark and Darcy. "We love you. We have been watching you. You are a loving and strong woman. Your beauty and education are your assets. Add to these your strong, loving nature and your career, and there are more assets."

Nark and Darcy successfully convinced Helen to forgive Eric's sexual affairs. Eric's mother Susan's love played a major role, too.

Helen saw herself in a dream again running away, but she never succeeded. Eric held Helen and kissed her.

The voice said, "Helen, you are born a woman because of Eric. You cannot run away. It is time to do the right thing. Helen, you are basically living to solve Eric's problems. Don't deny his love for you. He loves you."

This time, she understood the plot set in motion the time the voice began in her was beyond her control and must be something valuable. "Who entrusted this privilege?" she asked.

Eric jumped in and said, "I realized there aren't many friends to see and not too many places to visit. I chose to return to my base. This is my base. You are my base, Helen. No turning and running back."

This was beyond Helen's control. The marriage was the last thing on her mind but could she deny his love?

Eric looked at Helen and said, "Please come closer."

Eric was in tears. He asked, "Helen, please can we get married before another woman traps me again? We all believe marriage would drive them away. Please accept me. I'm your husband. The problem is just to make the marriage legal."

Helen had difficulty accepting the truth. She couldn't sleep: she tossed the whole night. Eric wanted to make love to her. She ignored him and left the bed.

A half an hour later, Helen walked back to the bed. She asked, "Eric, what is my future? You are a womanizer. I have too much to lose. You're too sexually active and too exposed to women. I can't pass your sexual test. I can't satisfy your love life. I love you, but I'm very much afraid."

Eric stood watching Helen, then said, "Look in my eyes and tell me you never did and never will love me. Tell me you haven't been in love with me all these years. I have waited for six years, Helen." Helen couldn't control her love for Eric any longer. She said, "If this is my destiny, we just have to face the truth. Yes, I can't run anymore." Eric rocked her to sleep.

Three weeks later, Eric and Helen were married in the Protestant Church. A large African circumcision party was held with all cultural rites. Having completed stages three and four, the marriage was then legalized. Eric became a new, happy, complete man with hope for a better future.

Two days later, Susan called Helen. She said, "My daughter Helen, remember I'm not just your mother-in-law. I'm ready to play the role of your mother. Helen, you have rights in our family. Take control and change Eric. We trust you can change him."

From that moment, Eric became Helen's first son, father, brother, and husband. Helen was the mother. Helen and Eric became one body. Eric called her Mom, Wife, and their nickname, Sweet. They moved to the big city, living in a two-bedroom apartment.

Eric said, "Thank you, Lord. I'm now a complete man."

African Marriage Code

1. The man presents himself to the parents of the woman he's interested in with gifts of liquor as a token of his intention to marry.
2. The interested man is presented to the community leaders and the parents' relatives. The suitor offers money and drinks to the community and presents clothes, shoes, head ties, and other gifts to the intended. From that time on, the community recognizes the man as the woman's suitor or husband-to-be.
3. The man pays the dowry to the intended's parents. After the payment of the dowry, she is recognized as his future wife. No man may touch her. If such harassment occurs, the offending party must pay a large sum of money to the injured party's family. The engaged man has exclusive rights to his future wife and her love.
4. The marriage contract combines Western tradition and African culture to be legally recognized. The marriage is registered for tradition's sake only, and the wedding ceremony includes the circumcision rite.

Chapter Thirteen

One bright afternoon, the house door was open when a stranger entered. He sat down without a word. Helen looked at him and asked, "Who are you?"

The man got up and asked, "Who are you? What are you doing here, Woman?"

Helen didn't answer. He moved up and down in the living room, very angry.

Helen watched his angry face, then said, "Man, my husband is not home. Can you leave a message?"

He looked at Helen, with even more anger, and shouted, "Who are you, Woman?"

Helen walked towards the wall so he could see better. He turned his face to the wall and saw the wedding photograph.

He looked and looked at her, then the picture. He asked, "Is that you?"

Helen said, "That is our wedding picture." Five minutes later, Helen said, "What do you want from my husband?"

He looked at Helen again and said, "So Eric is already married in the Church. Woman, you are too beautiful to be troubled. My daughter can't compete with you. Tell your husband that I came to collect, but it's over. He will never see me again. Good-bye."

Helen turned her head. She asked, "Collect what? We never owe late rent."

He looked at Helen and the photograph again, then said, "Woman, Eric is married in the Church. We lose the game."

"What game?" asked Helen.

"Just tell Eric a man was here to collect the money."

"What money, Man?"

"Eric will understand, Woman," he replied, then, crossing to the doorstep, he said, "I wish you were my daughter." He turned and went away.

A month before, Helen had said, "Eric, buy us a radio and cassette player."

Eric had looked at Helen and said, "No money."

"Why, Eric?" asked Helen. "What did you do with our money?"

"No money," said Eric.

Helen didn't believe Eric. She had asked, "Do you mean a man can't provide his family a source of relaxation?"

"It's getting too late for dinner," said Eric.

Dinner was served, and he said, "Bear with me. Your standard of living is much beyond my pocket."

"Kindly use your next month's salary to buy our desire," said Helen. She gazed at Eric and laughed three times.

Eric knew something was wrong, but couldn't pinpoint the problem. Finally he said, "My wife, you never laugh in that manner without cause. What is troubling you?"

"Nothing, Eric," Helen answered. "Maybe too many people depend on our income. Can you explain?"

He kept looking at Helen, while avoiding the question.

Helen laughed again and sang, "Master, Master. Not all

men are worth being called master. But the kind, gentle, faithful and loving are called Master, Master. Some men are jokers and fools."

He looked at her and went to bed. Eric understood the song very well.

Three hours after the stranger had gone, Helen said, "Eric, you had a visitor today."

"A man?" asked Eric.

"How do you know?" she asked.

"You're innocent, my wife Helen. I realize it's high time to understand my financial responsibilities," answered Eric. She burned her tongue on the hot tea.

Eric said, "Helen, what did the man say?" Eric remained calm as he waited to hear her response. He played it cool, but did not have a happy face. He didn't cry, but his eyes were red. A few minutes later, tears started dripping from his eyes.

She said, "Eric, you're crying."

"He came to collect money, Helen," Eric said.

Helen started crying, too. "The man said he would never come back."

Eric jumped from the bed, and shouted, "Oh God, thank you. You too, Helen."

She watched Eric jumping up and down like a baby and asked, "Why are you thanking me?"

"Yes, my parents and relatives are right. He will never come back. You have solved my problem. Now it is my turn to offer an explanation. I am now released from my anger and frustration. Thank you! Thank you! We have won the first battle. A big battle. Thank you!"

Helen didn't understand Eric, so she said, "Eric, tell me what that man came for."

Eric took a step closer to her., and she quickly sensed something wrong, but Eric laughed. He said, "Being married to you, Helen, is my blessing. I hope you believe my story."

Helen asked, "Is another woman pregnant again?"

Eric looked at Helen, then said gently, "Helen is too beautiful, kind and loyal to be treated like a child. You never asked me for your money. How many women in our society give their salaries to their husbands?"

Eric said, "Your money is gone."

"Gone where?" asked Helen.

"It's the most I can tell you now," he replied. "I admit I basically went over our income. That's the truth, Helen."

Helen quickly understood that Eric was in trouble. She looked at him and went out for fresh air. Ten minutes later he called, "Sweet, come inside." He said, "Please sit down. You deserve to hear the truth. Your lifestyle is going to be a mess. Please, we are one. Help me. I shall change."

She asked, "Is there another woman since we got married in the Church?"

Eric was ashamed to talk. The pride of having illegitimate children vanished. He saw the reality of life, and said, "If you were with me, all those women would not have trapped me with their children."

Helen quickly answered, "Blame yourself, I have nothing to do with your dirty life, Eric. Knowing my goals in life, you tempted me to quit school and devote my life to mothering you and your children.

"I have my own life, style of life, and my education. I'm not one of those dead wood." She continued, "You can't meet my standard of life. Are you asking me to change my lifestyle to support your love affairs?"

"I'm asking you to help me solve my problems," said Eric.

"Can you tell me the truth now, Eric?" asked Helen.

At that moment, he suppressed his male ego and stood up to tell the truth.

He said, "My third illegitimate child has two fathers. The other man is my friend. When my ex-mistress got pregnant, she never accepted I was the father. But her mother insisted I'm the father. She preferred me to my friend. The grandmother kept the child for a fee. I became their financial and romantic support. Even uneducated women want their lifestyle to be good. I was made to pay five hundred dollars monthly. When the baby was two months old she was married to my friend and went to live in the big city."

Helen never spoke a single word. Eric continued, "Helen, very few women share your theories, lifestyle, or your purpose in a committed love relationship. Your helping us, to believe in one another to grow up with love and become whole, and to support each other financially, morally and emotionally will produce a real, ever-loving relationship."

Eric asked, "What can we do to change women like my ex-mistress's mother, who use their daughters as a means to achieve their financial security?"

Helen looked up and answered, "Eric, see, our wedding photo is one of the answers. The man saw them and he will never come back. He can now collect money from your friend."

"Fortunately, you are pregnant. Children from out of wedlock are no more in my book. I have a successful and productive life with my wife," said Eric.

Helen felt there must be a way to protect children better, so she asked, "Eric, how can we change our society, the men and women who move from woman to woman and man to man?" Then she said again and again, "Now I can understand why Daddy never wanted another daughter. My daddy said a woman is worthless.

"It seems our lifestyles and values have shifted from hard work between a husband and wife and the old rules of having good morals. Enduring relationships between partners seem to have crumbled," said Helen. "Most men believe women shouldn't even have a career."

"That's true, they do," said Eric.

Helen asked, "Eric, do you have a suggestion?"

Eric said, "He will not come back. The marriage blessed in the Church proves illegitimate children have no room or a life in such homes. I won the game because there was no marriage before you," said Eric. "They can't prove my affairs with their daughters."

"Oh, darling," said Helen. "You should take a blood test because it is bad to throw children away. Are you not going to train them? You're wicked, Eric. You made love to their mothers. It takes two people to make a baby. Know it from me, you owe them their education. You helped to create problems for them and for us. We have to train them. You can't have it both ways. The children need good nurturing."

Helen continued to hammer into Eric a sense of good nurturing, saying, "A life that is honestly pursued is always on the right path. We shall train them."

Eric said, "With your support, Helen, we shall train them. Know it from me, they have nothing to gain from me but their education. Who knows the number of fathers they have. There is always one mother, but there could be many fathers."

"Tomorrow is another day, Eric," said Helen. "Today they are your sons.

"Once my children can read and write their names, I shall teach them the value of being themselves. Having the right educational goals provides status and pride. I shall do what is possible to discourage my son from having illegitimate children."

Later Helen was blessed with four daughters, one son and one step son.

Eric laughed with one eye closed, then he said, "You can never tell how your son is going to turn out."

Helen said, "I don't care what you do to your life, but I care for my children's future. Education first, Eric."

"Eric, good nurturing starts from early childhood. My son's life must never include illegitimate children. His success will come from helping others, his profession, practice, family relationships, and a stable marriage of loving one wife and their own children. "The father's property inherited without the child's education will never last.

"Eric, my mother taught me to be myself, trust myself, and work hard. A good education is the answer. You never listened to your mother until you started smelling like a rotten fish."

Eric looked at her and said, "I can understand you are mad at me."

Paul came in and sat down, so Eric and Paul drank beer. One hour later, Paul said, "We heard you are very helpful, Helen. Eric is very lucky. We appreciate your support in cleaning up Eric's mess. Very few women are willing to understand this problem."

The next day, Eric told Helen, "There is something you don't know and will not understand. There won't be any property for my children to share. Education is their property. Whatever we have belongs to us. You know too much, Helen."

Eric continued, "I don't know who is your guide, but you really know too much. Who are you? You know and understand most problems step by step. Do you have a manual in your brain? With something as important as having a successful marriage, solutions are already in your mind. Who is your best model?"

"Abigail, from the Bible, a wise woman is my role model. The other Bible characters add more daily," Helen replied. Then she laughed and said, "Eric, childhood learning and listening does register in the brain when the mother has her children's interests at heart.

"Children learn to suppress and deny what they hear. When the time comes, your brain will recall your parents' forbidding expressions, anger and their teaching not to trust anyone.

"The message might be different, Eric, but whatever the message is, the obedient child remembers the experience and the wounds. Also, children repress the pleasure they feel. Children's future life plans are formed from lessons learned in childhood." Eric listened to her words of wisdom.

Helen continued, "The price of obedience is sometimes

a loss of wholeness. But love gives us another chance for wholeness. Wholeness brings the feelings of true love to a relationship. The deepest purpose of love is to help us grow and bring a lovely life from infancy to marriage, manhood and womanhood to one another."

Eric continued to listen to her words of wisdom, then he said, "Sweet, you are like my mother. I can now understand why she loves you. Yes, I married a woman like my mother."

"My darling, this discussion gives us the opportunity to heal old wounds." Helen replied. "It brings wholeness again." He gazed at her and felt useless as a partner.

"We all have parents, but mine never taught me so early about life. Helen, your mother really loved you. "

"That is good nurturing," he acknowledged.

Eric laughed and said, "I wish she were alive now. Many people have said your mother was very loving and kind. You are the ripe fruit she produced."

Helen said, "I feel a person with whom one falls in love must progress towards an ever-loving marriage. When one changes from the past wrong doing, the old wound could be healed with new changes. Surely good feelings can be restored. But do we fully change, Eric?

"Knowing what I know now, not many educated women could go for you, Eric. My sister would never talk to you like this. I'm only worried about what you need to give in order to heal your heart. Heal you, Eric, from your dirty sexual affairs. You never listened to your parents, Eric. You are now going to listen to me. Do you hear me, dear Eric?"

Helen continued to wash Eric with the truth of life. She believed that men and women having sexual affairs were still in the darkness. She said, "If women could only discover each other's plans in life, what their behavior does to good men, the future of those fatherless children, and their own status in the society, men and women would learn not to act carelessly with each other."

Eric sorrowfully said, "I'm very sorry, Helen. I'm your husband, not a child."

"You're acting like my son, Eric," she came back. "I'm doing my job, so hear me out. Tell me, Eric, how can we understand each other's inner wounds?"

Eric said nothing, but was ready to listen.

Helen said, "Your mother asked me to change you. Are you ready for the change? Do you want your old life back? Are you happy? Why did you do this to me if you love me?"

Eric answered, "I can't change the past, but I can stop having affairs. Tell Mama I can, Helen. She wants you to teach me the truth of life. Tell her you are playing your part. All is fine; I'm happy."

But Helen did not stop. She hoped Eric's ego would commit to progress in life instead of having affairs and committing sexual sin, so she said, "Eric, we should understand as adults that there is a larger picture behind making love and having children. If we do, the pain would help us to decide the course of action to take with each other. It would control our inner feelings of love, affection, and passion."

"That's true," said Eric with shame and guilt.

Helen went on, "Many couples initially resist their ideas and feelings until words gather like sand. When a man becomes a secret alcoholic, or obsessive about his career, he is not there for his wife when she needs him most. The inner wound must be healed."

Helen felt the embarrassment of poverty that is facing the family. She felt that now was the time to heal their wounds. Eric's wounds must be healed if the family was to have a happy life.

She asked herself, Can I learn to love, value, and accept this part of him? The part I now hate? The part that makes him different from me? Can I trust he will not repeat loving other women?

Helen shouted, "Oh, small voice, is this where you landed me? Answer me, small voice!"

The voice said, "You will be able to love, value and accept every part of him. The part that cries out, 'I'm the right man for you. Look at me, please, and heal my wounded.'"

Eric and Helen told each other the different wounds in their lives from childhood. After that, they knew and understood what they wanted from each other instead of finding themselves in power struggles. They were stuck together in a loving relationship like innocent children again.

Eric cried for joy, then he said, "Helen, my father never loved me. He had money. He spent his money on my brother and his relatives. He sent my brother to high school. Only my mother trained me through high school."

Helen laughed and Eric asked, "Why are you laughing, Helen?"

Helen said, "Eric, my father abandoned me because I was born a woman. He told my mother, 'Take her, Rebecca. I need no more girls in my family.' He really rejected me. My mother sent me to school just before her death."

Eric and Helen figured out that each was fearful of abandonment so they hugged each other.

She said, "It takes more than communication skills, to listen and respond. It takes love and relationships. It takes the forgiveness to build up a loving, equal partnership, sharing and working together. It isn't about having many children and crazy lovemaking. It is about passion, love and truth. It isn't about control and female slavery, but freedom of expression and decision-making." Helen and Eric lived in the same world with joy and happiness.

Helen taught Eric the true role of a man and a woman. Feeling rejected vanished from their lives, and Eric became a loving husband. Helen was strong and obedient. She respected Eric and made smart decisions though she was a woman.

Chapter Fourteen

Two years later, Eric said, "Helen, it is fine and okay for you to hate my messy life and to create new changes in me. Really it is okay." He continued, "Never be afraid you are going too far. It even makes sense that you felt threatened by my uncaring behavior. I can tell from your eyes it reminds you of your father's second marriage."

"Eric," said Helen, "You are right; can you really see what you have done to our lives?"

"Yes, I can," he replied. "I can understand much of the frustration you feel inside, when we spend all your money to maintain this home, to avoid what you perceive as chaos."

"Is that what you are feeling about me?" asked Helen.

Eric looked at her and answered, "Yes."

Helen asked, "Is this just a game of shame and feeling sorry? Do you really understand the effect of what you have done? Do you understand how pained I sometimes feel that you didn't keep yourself holy for me? Do you know you are nicknamed? And your relatives are calling you names."

Eric said, "Darling, you are the everlasting wife. My life is yours, yours is mine. Make it work now while we still have a chance to work together. Let's forget the past, then move forward for a better future."

Eric laughed and said, "Helen, I heard you when you said it is only me who knows where to put that stuff. Remember, my darling, you have proved there are other ways to live besides my way. I also heard you saying that you don't like the fact that I keep things from you."

Helen said, "I hope you got it, Eric." They both got it and smiled.

Helen turned to face Eric and said, "Sometimes when we fall in love, we never understand why and how. We can fall in love not because the loved one is handsome, sensitive, beautiful and kind, but because his or her love reminds us of our lost childhood."

"Helen, there are different stages couples and love partners pass through," Eric interjected. "As the romantic love disappears, frustrations and disappointment in our partners appear. Many of us despair and disappear.

"Our mates or partners begin to look like strangers. We forget when we used to see them as elegant, when they seemed so reasonable and so open. Many men and women give up too soon and just check out."

She said, "Eric, do you think one can change? What is the devil? Why is the devil governing this earth? Nobody is above temptation. Likewise, nobody is above forgiveness and change."

Eric looked at her with his mouth wide open, but did not say a word. He was waiting for more.

Helen continued, "Men and women simply never tolerate the distance and disappointment our partners bring to us. We begin to look for better and legitimate excuses to avoid connecting with our partners. Sometimes these excuses are really the gateways out of our closeness, but they can also play the role of a real gateway to build our love if we stick around to solve the problems."

Helen waited and worked very hard to solve Eric's problems. That was the role of Helen. She was a good homemaker, a professional, modern woman, a mother and a businesswoman. She used music sometimes to call Eric home. She was also a good listener and adviser. These traits also provided immediate gratification. While others used them to avoid intimacy between partners, Helen encouraged them as a means of sharing intimacy with her husband.

It took two months to understand Helen's program. One Saturday afternoon, Eric came home for lunch with a male visitor. He watched Helen for a good twenty minutes, then he said, "Helen, are we going to have fresh fish?"

"How do you know that?" she asked.

"I must see before I believe," the visitor said.

"See what and believe what?" asked Helen.

"I have seen one activity," he replied

"What activity?" asked Helen.

He was astonished. He said, "You are washing Eric's clothes with your hands. Where is your housemaid? Answer me, Helen. Are we going to eat fresh fish?"

She laughed, then went to the kitchen where the food was ready. Lunch was served, and the menu consisted of fresh fish, soup with lots of green vegetables, okra, yam, slices of pineapple, and mango fruit.

He enjoyed the meal, then he stood up and said, "Eric, you are really in earthly heaven. Some of us are not married yet."

"Have you seen with your eyes?" asked Eric.

"That's not all Eric," said the visitor. "I ate with my mouth."

Eric said, "Tell me, friend, do you think you could afford to come home late? There is a bell in my head, and it rings when its time to be home, where Helen is waiting, food is waiting. Hearing this, I run home like a little child before it is too late. She is my mother, not just a wife."

The visitor watched Helen and asked, "Who are you woman? Do you have another sister?"

Helen laughed and said, "Why are you asking so many questions about me and my sister?"

He said, "The good ones don't talk and fight," then he explained, "Helen, Eric said you were going to cook freshwater fish today, so we must hurry home for lunch."

Eric added "Yes, I told him so. Before I left the house today, you said, 'Today is market day.' We eat freshwater fish every market day. Am I wrong, Helen?"

The visitor said, "Woman, you are too good to cook. Eric knows your menu. Tell me, do you have a sister like you?"

"The one you call my maid is my sister," she answered.

"Is she a good cook like you?" asked Eric's friend.

Helen answered, "You are married!" They laughed.

When activities are used as an escape, as a means of imbalance in equality and slavery, they take the energy out of the relationship. Energy that would much better be used for mutual healing is sometimes abused.

Eric used Helen's energy for healing his emotions and former affairs. Eric understood the role of love and what love could produce. He said, "Friend, she is my mother. She holds the key to our progress. She is a good planner and operator. My role is to support her."

The man gazed at Helen and said, "We wish your mother was still alive to see how well you turned out. Helen, you are a loving, caring woman, and a dear wife."

Eric laughed and tried to hide his joy. He said, "Friend have you ever seen a woman of our time rendering her salary to her husband? She gave me all. Knowing she is the best manager, I gave all back to her. She manages the family and pays the children's school fees. That is the truth. Do you think I deserve her? This is God's blessing. Helen is my blessing."

Helen called for Eric, and said, "Before we begin our activities as a means of existence, try to decide what real existence means in the life of partners."

Eric said, "A real existence produces good results."

Chapter Fifteen

One evening, Helen gave her salary to Eric, and he said "Thank you,"

During the family management discussion, Helen said, "Eric, I need $200 from my salary."

"For what, Helen?" he asked.

Helen said, "For a wrapper and a head tie. You know there is a big party next weekend."

"Yes, a big party," agreed Eric.

"Remember, Eric, we must attend," said Helen. "And this time, Eric, we must dress to show our status."

Ten minutes later, Eric said, "Helen, the family needs the money more. Use your old clothes, for the party."

She said, "Eric, you know my class. My old clothes are outdated. I'm talking about my money, not yours, Eric. For sixteen years, I have lived your life. Now I want to be myself. The real Helen Brown, Eric. I want my life back. Do you understand me, Eric?" Helen begged Eric for the money.

Eric said, "Yes, Helen, you changed your lifestyle for

my sake, for the family's sake, and for our children, Kate, Alice, Peace, Sarah, Justine, and Solo that are in school, but please don't buy the wrapper."

"I'm very sorry, Eric," said Helen. "What you do with your money is up to you, but this money is mine, too."

"Not this month, Helen," said Eric. "You are not dressing for others, but for me, your husband."

Helen laughed again and again, then said, "Sorry, Eric, I dress for myself, not for you. I have my body and my status. I'm not of your low standard of life."

Thinking she knew of a way to solve the problem, Helen ran downstairs. She said, "Nark, talk to your brother. He refuses to give me $200 out of my salary to buy a wrapper for the party. Talk to him, Nark. We never quarrel or fight. This is going to change our lives and marriage into a new phase." While telling herself she was doing the right thing, she was interrupted by Nark who never wanted his brother's progress.

Nark looked at Helen, then he said, "Very well, Helen. You don't understand that all your money belongs to your husband?"

Helen was shocked. She said, "All my money belongs to a man? Are you telling me all my money belongs to Eric?"

Helen was furious. She said, "Nark, know from today that I am not a slave!" She ran upstairs and went to the bedroom, crying.

"Oh, my darling, why are you crying?" asked Eric. Helen could not talk as she was shaking and trembling.

Eric was afraid watching her.

"What is wrong? Tell me," he said.

The fear made her feel like a stranger in her own house, and she said, "I pity you, Eric. I can't forget what Nark said."

"Don't cry because of a wrapper, Helen," he said, but Helen was still furious.

Eric already knew the answer, so he said, "I guess Nark didn't support you."

"Not just like that, Eric," she answered. "It is not that simple, Eric. Men are bad. Nark made me recover myself today."

Eric was crushed. He believed his brother was going to break up his marriage, so he sorrowfully said, "My wife, please come."

Helen was sad, and she said, "All our money belongs to you, " Is that true, Eric?"

"That's not true," he said. "Nark's wife never supported his family, so he is jealous of me. My whole family is always saying that I am very lucky. You are a wonderful woman. Their jealousy can't mess and change our lives. Take the money. I'm very sorry, Helen," Eric apologized. "Never trust a brother-in law, my wife. They can be jealous, too."

Back in the bedroom, Eric found her very fussy and crying a lot. He said, "Sweet, it makes sense that you would feel rejected, angry, out of control and terrible. You are not a slave in our home." He reached over, touched her cheek, and kissed her in gratitude.

"I'm angry at you, Eric," she fumed."You made me feel as if I don't value my children and the future of our family. Is that right?"

And Helen a loving hardworking kind wife not wanting to disgrace her husband, desired to put Nark's jealousy and bad feelings away secretly loving her husband again.

This event happened when Eric was still under the control of his relatives as most men like Eric are. While very few women are like Helen because heartbreak is a very serious disease facing most families and most women.

She finally put the jealously behind to rest with a just but very kind plan. "You are the man, from now on, bring home part of your salary. From now on, I shall buy whatever I want with my money. You have no right to control my money any longer, Eric."

This became a bad incident for Eric and Helen because of Nark's opinion, jealousy and control.

Thereafter, she clothed the whole family, supervised the look of their apartment and Eric with her own money. Their appearance matched their educational status and values.

Eric said, "Oh, brother, you made me lose control of my family. Frustration is back in my life. For the past two nights, I have walked helplessly and nearly fell down. Slowly I began to walk down the road, hoping I'm in control and heading home. My head was throbbing painfully as I got closer to home."

After contemplating, his heart yearn to respond to emotions again, but again feeling dirty inside.

Three weeks later, he rested his head against Helen, and she asked, "What do you want, Eric? This is your fault, too. I knew Nark was troubled and jealous because of my university education, but you would not hear my soft voice. My peacefulness made you complacent. Never think I am a lowlife human like you. There is no turning back. I promise to use my money very well for the family. I'm unlike you, Eric."

Eric said, "Please listen and hear me out."

"Oh no, leave me alone," Helen ordered. "That is my last decision."

Eric said, "From today, we are dropping the training of Nark's children in the high school. That is his reward for messing up my life."

Helen looked forlorn and said, "Our hearts yearn to respond to God's creation. Hopefully my heart will be warm and inviting so that when you do call, a worthy place will always be waiting."

Two months later, Eric called to Helen, and he said, "I wish we could pick up the training of my uncle's son, who is in the higher institution. Do you know him?"

"Yes, his mother was very nice to me when I was a

teacher in your town," Helen acknowledged. "Yes, he can replace Nark's children." What bad luck Nark.

Eric smiled and said, "Thank you. What would I do without you, Helen? This is perfect. I am deeply moved because you supported me instead of attacking." He kissed her and smiled. Eric joyfully drove out.

Helen laughed, then she said, "Well done, Eric. This is a better gateway. We are equal partners." She took her car and went shopping.

Chapter Sixteen

Six months later, Eric was still growing, but he was still missing his past life of premarital sexual freedom. Now, instead of taking pride in his status he was called a man without power.

One of Eric's relatives said, "Helen, you are a fool. How do you expect a man who has children in all corners of the world to have means and luck for progress? The souls of those unmarried women are hurting him." Helen didn't defend Eric.

He continued, "Eric is a womanizer. The family is ashamed of him. We feel and believe his life and progress are threatened. I am embarrassed and absolutely have steamed him out of my system and plans."

Helen turned her back, then said, "That's not true. Is he not your uncle?" Helen laughed and added, "Eric acted like a primitive man. He made the mistake of accepting some of those children. He also went with women who consider children their sexual solution to poverty."

He looked at Helen, then asked, "When are you going to open your eyes and your ears? Helen, better you should hear the truth from Eric's best friends."

"On the contrary, Paul is a liar," Helen countered.

"We know you must defend Eric," said his relative, "but his love is blinding you from the truth, Helen. Eric is a very lucky man to have you. Can you change him, Helen?"

Helen did not hesitate. She said, "Look well, man. The behavior the elders handed down has spread all over society. The modern man never wanted to be left out, so he took control. Some men never wanted many wives but only illegitimate children to achieve social status. They can then drink with the left hand."

"Go home, Helen," said Eric's relative. "You never see the truth. Eric is always right in your eyes. We hope you will change him one day. You're too good for him. You are his blessing, Helen."

While Helen was with Eric's relative, Eric was drinking with his friends. His friend Paul got up, stood before his friends and said, "Who can drink with his left hand?"

Eric said, "You know you can't. You're not a complete man!" They all laughed.

Eric took the drink and shouted, "I'm a man, a complete man." He drank with his left hand. They all clapped their hands and shouted, "You are a real complete man, Eric. You made it all, but you have no money yet. Until you have money, Paul is the highest man here in our group and the community."

Paul said, "Children from out of wedlock never count anymore. These modern times, money counts. Sit down, Eric. I'm number one. Children from lovers are bad dreams."

Eric became sad. His education didn't help him get ahead. His friend, Paul was a millionaire, and his jealousy became very destructive to Eric's ego. He simply tolerated the difference between himself and Paul.

When he returned home, Eric looked at Helen and said, "You are my blessing."

"Listen, Eric," Helen came back, "it is time for the next

stage, for we have different goals in life. I have waited patiently for the Lord all these years. He has started to listen to me and heard my cry. He brought me up out of the point of destruction and set my feet upon a rock, making my foot- steps very firm. Set your heart to study the words of God and put the truth of His words into action. God will certainly hear your prayer. Your personal commitment is very vital to your progress, our progress, Eric."

He sat still and looked depressed. He didn't smile and refused to talk to the children. Eric felt moody and dissatisfied with his life.

Helen shook her head, held Eric and said, "Many times, the voice for mercy echo in me like cool water offered in love. God's great mercy and covenant to his children who truly repent, the tender mercy of God would bestow Salvation from depression and poverty. God's mercy reaches every one who believes and in all corners of the world. There's kindness in His justice and healing power in His blood.

"There is purification and riches in His love. Our lives would seem clearer and less tangled. Come from the wilderness and let God's solitude strengthen our souls. We can then hear His voice, can sense his calling for us and we can then see His surprises in sunrise."

Eric only listened waiting for more.

Helen walked to him and said, "Eric, I can't believe another year has passed. Time goes faster than we think. The children grow faster than we expect. I don't know anyone close to us who never talks. No one who never plays and tries to be a role model in his family." Eric didn't say a word but just looked at Helen again and again.

It was heartbreaking to see Eric continuously drifting away from the children because of money. She felt so alone and so vulnerable when she traveled on business trips. She said, "How can I travel when Eric still hurts with his past and empty bank account."

Eric never wanted to talk about anything, he just kept to

himself, lying on the sofa watching TV. His depressed feelings deprived the children of his closeness and fatherly activities with them. Love wasn't expressed or in action. He only smiled if the children's school report and results arrived. He would look at his daughters and smile for their good work.

Helen watched him. She said, "Eric, the children are wondering why I married you and had them." He did not say a word.

One of the afternoons when Eric was out, Helen's stepson Solo, said, "Mama, what is wrong with Daddy? He never plays with us anymore like a father. Maybe Daddy has too many children."

"Who gave you these ideas?" asked Helen.

"Daddy cries when you are not at home," said Solo. "He is hiding something from you, Mama. Ask him. We believe he will tell you because you love him."

Helen said, "Son, maybe he is unhappy because I refused to give him money to repair his car."

"That is not all, Mama," said Solo. "We heard he is not on good terms with his best friend, the millionaire. Paul is your relative, Mama."

Helen said, "Solo, Daddy is a well-educated man, that's what counts. He has a name. He can get a job anywhere in this world. We're proud of him."

Solo said, "Tell daddy that we love him very much. and we shall try to be well educated like Daddy and Mama."

Helen whispered this to Eric, and he smiled, but then took his car and went out and did not return until 2:00 a.m.

The past continued to hurt him, and the children continued to see Helen getting hurt by their father's behavior.

One evening when Eric was out, the children said, "Mama, don't wait for him. Learn to eat without Daddy. When he comes, give him cold food. Tell him we had no gas to warm the food." Eric started eating cold food.

Two months later, Helen was wakened to a very familiar reality. She knew Eric's old habit was hurting him. He was unhappy and encouraged by friends to start drinking again.

Helen tapped her brain for a solution. She looked at Eric and said, "Eric, your friends and relatives are your enemies and your murderers. One day, you will find your bed empty and lonely. You will be your own cook. Blame yourself, Eric."

Chapter Seventeen

Helen confidentially talked to men and women who had premarital affairs. Their stories were almost the same as Eric's. They felt conflict, guilt, and were filled with secrets. They found life very difficult to live with one woman or man.

She found that men had not been aware of the loss of couple passion and friendship with their wives. The rights of marriage and secrets of couple love were never understood among a cheating society. Most women felt no different, but had more responsibilities and guilt. They were viewed as man-snatchers.

The interviews and talks revealed a touching story of men and women living in the shadows and losing their way to a better life.

What they lost was not the ability to have many women, men and children. They lost the capacity for desire and pleasure with a wife or husband. The majority of these men and women never found the pleasure. Having many children was their only gateway to a better life.

Marriage, as people know, has a silent side. The inner

voice says, "This is me. I know what I want. I understand what it means. I can think right and now I am making the right choice. I know what I need and feel, how I behave, and how I am responsible for my actions."

Instead, these cheating men are saying, "Maybe I wasn't aware of what I was doing. I don't know what is wrong, I just don't feel like me anymore. My friends are doing it, so I have to follow. My wife is beautiful but not interested in our bed. One woman is like eating the same food daily. My wife can't support me. She is not the woman that I married. The society encourages and permits affairs with other women and men. If my wife sleeps with another man, she must go back to her parents. I love her, but can't stop seeing other women. I need children out of wedlock like my friends. In most societies, more married men than married women have affairs."

The women say that as wives they feel frozen, half dead, like shadows on ice or automatic pilot, and pretty terrible. They are depressed and silent. Their rate of depression is higher than single women who have affairs with married men. They feel more anxiety, low self esteem, and incompetent to care for the family and the children. If something is going wrong in the marriage, these types of women are very eager to get out to save their health.

Helen wondered, "Why is marriage harmful to some women?" She talked about this with Eric.

"From generation to generation women are taught that marriage is the best thing that can happen to a woman," Helen said."Likewise, men are taught by their elders that they have the right to move from woman to woman because they are the head of the family. Women are nothing. Women should depend on their husbands and brothers.

"But, in most marriages all over the world, most women and children depend on the woman's income, care and guidance.

"The moment women are married, they are destined to become selfless. Marriage as an institution has never kept women entirely. There has been no room for the pleasure that is loving and outspoken. Frankly, women who feel as entitled to their own needs and desires as the rest of the family are put down.

"Woman has been traditionally called, and is still called, selfish. This is bad from a woman's point of view, although all children belong to women. Remember that, Eric.

"Most men and women describe themselves as happily married, so having an affair must be kept secret. They hide their moods from their partners in order to make life go smoothly."

Helen looked at Eric and continued, "With her lover, a woman feels very free to do and be whatever she really wants and feels at that moment. That is the basis of the closeness. These women still believe that their husbands get the better part of them when they are easier and less moody. Husbands and lovers must remember to be nice and good to women because female sexuality dies when there is no freedom, only slavery.

"Staying sexually alive in a marriage relationship is not about sex as such. It is about having freedom to be one's self. It is your creativity, your vitality, and yourself. It is you, all you can give and honestly express."

Helen added, "Remember to tell the truth if you need help to protect your life and status. One day, lies could catch up with you, Eric.

"Anyway, marriage is good for only the good wives who are not selfish women. Such women take care of everyone."

While Helen was busy working hard to promote Eric's name, others, including his relatives, gathered to stop Eric's progress.

A tale of dark hours, days and months was in store for Helen and her two daughters, Sarah and Kate.

While Eric was in the university, Helen was a high school teacher. One Sunday afternoon, after a church service, Debra Cator, Eric's ex-mistress dropped in at Helen's apartment, and Helen was terrified. Why would Debra visit her? Helen asked, "What do you want, Debra? You are not a friend. Why are you here? This is my apartment."

Debra said, "Helen, you know why I'm here. Can't you see me? You know what is going on, don't you?"

"Tell me why you are here," Helen demanded.

Debra asked, "Where is my son?"

Helen answered, "Your son, has not visited us for three days."

Debra laughed and said, "Helen, remember he is my son, and he's Eric's first son."

Helen smiled deeply, then said, "I understand all too well, Debra."

Eric's sister came in, and said, "Debra, we don't need you here. This is Helen's apartment. Eric has nothing here. Your son came, ate, and left two hours ago, when Helen was not home. Leave Helen alone. She is the most kind, generous woman we have in our family."

Debra said, "Helen, give me Eric's address."

"Oh, no," said his sister. "Helen can't give you my brother's address. Don't write to him. He's married to Helen, the woman we love. We don't love you. Get out of Helen's house."

Eric's sister tried to push Debra out, but Helen and Debra started to fight.

Helen said, "Sorry, Debra. Better wait until Eric is home during Christmas."

Debra asked, "Don't you know you're training Eric for me and my son?"

Helen said, "I'm training Eric for our family. Eric is the head of a family that includes your son, but not you, Debra."

"Helen, I am here to warn you," Debra challenged.

"Warn me about what, Debra?"

"Stop training Eric at the university," said Debra.

Helen laughed and said, "This is amazing. You want me to stop training my husband?"

"Yes," said Debra. "I am not alone. Others sent me to warn you. If you don't stop the training, there will be a war between you and our group."

"Your dark group," said Helen. "You can't stop me, Debra."

The sister shouted, "You wicked woman, carry your troubles away! Find a man to marry."

"Why are you protecting Eric?" asked Debra. "We are going to seek revenge for this horrible role Helen is playing. Immediately Helen will be destroyed. She must never have a son."

Debra gazed at Helen, then said again, "Remember Solo is not your son. You labor for us. We understand Helen is two months pregnant," she explained.

Helen said, "You can't succeed, Debra. God is my judge and my guide. Go with your dark acts, I know you are the source of my troubles."

Helen was determined to make Debra see the truth and thwart her plans. She said, "Only God can scatter the power of wicked men."

Chapter Eighteen

Three days later, the darkest hour arrived. About 10:00 p.m., Kate started crying and screaming.

On the morning of the following day, the sister found ants and snakes covering all the food in the kitchen. She raised the alarm and shouted to Debra, "You are a wicked woman. You can't drive Helen away." Helen and Eric's sister brought hot water from a friend's house and poured it. The water killed some of the ants and snakes. The rest escaped.

The sister and Helen threw all the food away, but on the third night, the ants and snakes came back. Kate continued crying at night and refused to eat the food from the kitchen.

The ants and snakes continued to come for one month. Helen fed Kate with milk and baby foods. She stopped walking for ten months although there was nothing wrong with her. She was afraid the snakes and ants would bite her.

The snakes continued to come during the day. Helen understood the message, but she continued to pray for Eric's progress. Her prayers were in Eric's heart.

Three weeks after Debra's visit, Helen received a letter from Eric, who wrote, "Last night, I woke up and found myself on the floor. Please Helen, tell my mother that three women came to me in a dream. They told me never to go to town. My next visit home would be my last. I should not return to the university. Please Helen, pray for me."

Helen and Eric's mother, fasted and prayed for seven days. On the seventh day, a snake appeared from nowhere and came within a few inches of biting Helen's leg. She killed the snake and the sister burned it.

The next morning, another woman stood by the doorstep and said, "Helen, Eric and your children will never progress. Helen, you never knew what happened to your mother. You will join her sooner than expected."

As the dark war continued, a woman stranger came, and said to Helen, "My daughter, we see, hear and understand. You will never be alone. Your cry will soon be answered. Give me one hundred dollars and don't ask any questions." The stranger went away.

One week later, Kate started eating and walking and Helen was transferred to a better school.

Eric had a car accident on his way home from the university, and he was sick for seven days. After that, Eric's mother never allowed Eric to spend holidays in his town. Helen's town became Eric's home.

One year later, Helen had a son, and Eric named him Peace. Eric said, "Helen, you have given me male and female children. We won again. You are a perfect wife."

Helen said, "Being a perfect wife is the killer of woman's pleasure. For pleasure depends on selfishness and being one's self, the ability to insist on what is good for one's own needs.

"The world and the elders never talk about perfect men.

"They believe women are the property of men. Maybe there could be perfect men if men were taught to respect women."

The mother laughed, then said, "Helen, you're perfect

because you see the truth and follow it. You use your education, money and love for all, mostly those who tried to harm your family. These things place you above the wicked women."

"Susan, you're full of wisdom. Helen replied. I always wondered if Eric might have been a perfect man if not for his past. He never listened to anyone about women."

"You're right," said Susan. "Now he understands. Helen, there is hope Eric will change because the marriage institution has changed a great deal between the age of farming and the age of women's education. Men slowed women, but now men can't do that because men and women are equal and educated. But there is something we still have to do."

"What is that, Susan?" asked Helen.

Susan answered, "Helen, women in this modern age have sex before marriage, like men."

"Yes," said Helen, "that is part of women's right's and equality. Men can then understand they are not better than women.

"These women are well educated and hold higher level positions. They have good careers like men. They are self fulfilled and the sole family financial support, like those good men."

"Like Helen," said Susan. Helen looked at Susan and they both laughed.

Helen said, "Some people are saying it is too much for women to have such status because it's destroying marriage."

Susan shouted so loud that she nearly pulled the roof down, and many people gathered. "What's wrong, Susan?" they asked. "Are you fighting with Helen?"

"Oh no," answered Susan. "We're talking about perfect women."

Helen said, "Women's freedom is destroying the family because women will not be slaves anymore. But many women are still in need of help. For that reason, many men are urging women to return to their slave life. These men only want to support women's self-sacrificing. Sometimes, the bell of perfect wifehood rings in women's ears. Women are torn by the dilemma of selfishness as men see it."

Both men and women shouted louder than Susan. Many saying, "We wish our daughters could be like these educated women. Their children could live a better life."

Susan said, "Helen is not finished."

Helen continued, "This situation made modern women immobilized by guilt everyday, aspiring to become what they could never be."

"Helen is a perfect wife, mother and homemaker," said, Susan. "Now her role includes perfect wage earner, too."

"The old idea of goodness and respect for the mother's role hasn't gone away. It only became harder to live up to," said Helen.

One of the community's men said, "You're as good as any man, Helen. Eric is a very lucky man. But be ready. Many women and men are going to fight you. We heard you already faced a snake and ant war."

"Why?" asked Helen.

"It is so because you are too good for the competition," said the man. "Eric is not looking at them and listening to them anymore."

Helen said, "Man, one of the problems of modern times is how women try to live up to their ideal selves, to be good wives and mothers."

"No action is black and white," he replied. "Some people believe what we don't know or see has less effect on our emotions. That is why most men keep their wives at home, to avoid competition."

"That's true, Helen," said Nancy, Helen's friend. "We can now recognize the truth about why most women keep silent about previous sexual experiences. This helps if one has a jealous husband. When a woman finds the right man, whatever happened before the marriage is past. All the joy, love and pain suddenly seem irrelevant, sometimes even shameful. Such women are afraid to speak about their boyfriends and past love life to their mates. Such behavior prevents fear, hurt and jealousy.

"A real modern couple sees the past as the beginning of life. The wedding dress sometimes seems to clean the past," Nancy continued. "From the wedding, the woman's real sexual self starts to improve. She becomes someone new and better."

Helen said, "A man never forgets the past, especially when he has a son."

"That's true," Nancy agreed.

Helen said, "Nancy, it becomes a nightmare closing the road for a better future. The man is more of a dreamer than a real lover and husband. The war never ends.

"It's better we ask ourselves to explain our knowledge and sexual experience. That lessens our desire to be unfaithful," Helen said.

"It's much better if we keep ourselves holy waiting for our partners. This is the hardest thing for modern men and women to resolve. One day they will learn to wait after facing war."

Nancy said, "Helen, we are the modern women in modern times Both men and women get married with extensive sexual experience. Men have learned not to ask, 'Are you a virgin?' Likewise, women are not ready to say, 'I'm a virgin."

Helen laughed and said, "They are both trapped.

"What both partners do is to protect what they love. Maybe their egos need protection. This makes them appear a little better, but inside them, they hurt greatly."

Susan turned to Helen, who continued, "Women mostly live in silence and improve themselves to fit into the ideal. This way they protect their husbands' egos."

"That's true," said Susan, "but men never protect their wifes' egos. Men feel they have freedom to move from woman to woman."

"Nancy, there is too much knowledge in the modern world said Helen. Many people wonder, how do men and women improve their love after marriage? Most women feel uncomfortable talking about their desires."

"Why is that so, Helen, if we're all human like men?" asked Nancy.

Helen said, "That is wrong. Our bodies belong to us. We're all human beings. If men can talk about what they feel, women must talk the same about their desires. This way, husband and wife become one flesh."

Paul and his friend listened to the interesting topic, then Paul asked Helen why women stopped showing and telling men their desires.

"Most women feel that is too bold and too unlike a woman and that it is very threatening to demand their husband's love," Helen replied.

"Women refuse to say, 'Honey, this is how I like it. Here is what I want, need, touch, and touch me here and there; wait for me darling.' Rather, women are afraid. Women die in silence and stay obedient while the active men go out for the right action.

"Men feel they're the master, the leader of loving activities. If she wants it a way he hasn't tried before, he feels less manly. Some men would say, she is too advanced."

She said, "Paul, nothing will please such a man until he finds answers to these questions: 'Who taught her? Does she love me? Is he better than me?' Women silence themselves about their real feelings about caring and loving.

"This behavior is to protect their husband's vulnerability. Women keep quiet, refuse to take risks, but pull back sadly and suppress their loving desires.

"As the years go by, women's capacity and ability for pleasure almost vanish. Women begin to complain about having headaches.

"This doesn't mean women never want to make love. A perfect wife waits for the man to ask when the time is right and is satisfied with what the man knows how to do, but this behavior does not result in making love.

"When the pleasure dies, the real woman dies. The marriage turns to social status only. The main thing might even die, too, if there is no outside love affair," Helen concluded insightfully.

Paul screamed and rushed home to his family. Helen called, "Paul, you still have more to teach your wife." He turned back and listened.

Helen continued, "Women must remember that good communication dies when women are still protecting their husbands. The couples have nothing more in common than talking about the children, the house and work.

"There is no connection to make them reach out and say, 'Let's make love, darling; I love you, I need you now, tonight.' Never wait for a man to ask," said Helen. "Time might be running out. Time waits for no man.

"My sister women, being a man as we know it may make them much more vulnerable to having affairs. This is because the woman doesn't ask for what she wants and doesn't want.

"Ask your husband, and he will give you what you want. What he wanted is what he married; a woman with a voice, education, beauty, one who is hardworking, open-minded, free and equal.

"Never leave your children to a fast life, as such a life is nowhere. All men are the same. Ask; he will make you happy.

"I'm not asking men to go out and have affairs, but asking women to be free with their husbands and demand love from them when they need it.

"The desire will run out if women never ask. Ask, sister women. Show him your love desire. Never hide your feelings, because one can die in silence. Take from him whatever he can offer in truth and honesty," Helen again concluded.

Helen watched Eric for two days watching with the children. On the third day, she said, "Eric, sharing pleasure and forgiving transgression are two secrets of recovery from the past, but there is still another major point."

"What point?" asked Eric. "Say it now. I want to hear it."

"Telling me the truth, Eric," said Helen.

Eric asked, "Really? Do you want the truth, everything?"

"Yes, everything, Eric," Helen answered. He told Helen the truth and came alive.

From that moment of truth, Eric became whole again. He was his own therapist and was able to control his sexual feelings. Eric reduced his number of friends and his visits to his relatives. The marriage grew solid. Complete love took control.

Eric said, "Darling, lies were killing me and hurting our progress. I'm free. Freedom from lies can make us whole."

Helen watched Eric, then said, "Men and women are equal in the sight of God. Respect is due to those who deserve respect. Is Christ divided? Can we answer that the Maker made men only to be rich and famous? The grace of God is for all people. We must respect each other as human beings."

Eric said, "Remember, Helen, it is said and written, 'I will destroy the wisdom of the wise, and will bring to another the understanding of the prudent.' Where are the wise? Where are men and their wisdom? Do we all need freedom, respect and love? Men need to see women as equal partners. Fools are now trying to be wiser while the wise who fight for respect are becoming fools."

Eric became a converted man. He was very happy. He remembered the time before he became corrupted. He said, "The foolishness of God is wiser than men and the weakness of God is stronger than men. He that glories, let him glory in the Lord. Truly they glory in the Lord. Can I glory in the Lord, Helen?" he asked.

Helen answered, "Darling, you can if you keep the faith."

But, because family love is sometimes not enough for a man, Eric became depressed again. He wasn't happy because of his relatives and the townspeople, but he endured their rejection.

Her faith in God increased daily while watching for Eric. She looked at him and said, "God's generosity remains constant even when we turn away from Him. He has endless streams of acceptance and grace, even His tiny presence gives us joy.

"Though we shouldn't often complain, it is a relief just to understand He is there for us. This stream can turn us around through involuntary strength gripping us. We must push with all of our strength to overcome the enemy."

The weaker Eric became, the more Helen's Spiritual Power increased fighting for Eric's concentration on good life ahead.

You can't have a royal palace, the sumptuous home, even a real shelter residence, without humbly imagining the provincial setting can be provided in God's time and His terms not human terms.

Chapter Nineteen

Eric spent twenty years of his life helping to build the community he loved as secretary of the Community Development Union. After meeting with the youths, Eddie Martins, the Union speaker, and ten youth members they decided not to accept the two millionaire's Paul and his friends, financial plans. Eric thought the plan could create more poverty among the community dwellers.

Ten days later, another Community Development Union Meeting was held and there was a big showdown. The millionaires adorned with gold chains and beads, wore expensive wrappers with shoes to match. Eric also dressed well, but he had a nasty experience.

Doctor Eric was the most educated man in the community, an honest man who believed in the progress of the community as his own goal. He never used the community for his financial and personal gain. But such a man was not recognized by the elders. He served for twenty years, but had no money to buy social status.

The elders ordered no chairs or seats for Eric and his group. The elders said, "Sit on the floor. Who cares for your many degrees? Money counts, Eric."

Nark said, "We are ashamed of you, Eric."

Eric replied, "Elders, your dreams must never come true. I can't release the money. The money is the town's hope in time of trouble. Sitting on the floor is not the answer. Using the town's people and community's money for personal gain is wrong." Eric sat on the floor.

"I hope many of us will live long enough to see what this money will do for our community," he continued. "Sorry, I can't sign."

The humiliation of letting Eric sit on the floor raised an alarm among the people. The town started to panic. The youth surrounded Eric to fight the millionaires, who wanted to use the community for their personal gain. The meeting was adjourned.

That very night, the elders and their followers staged a battle to eliminate Eric and Eddie, the union speaker.

A madman ran in and shouted, "Run! Run away to the next town. They're coming to kill you tonight, Eddie."

Twenty minutes later, three men with guns surrounded Eddie's house. They searched the whole house, but never found Eric and Eddie.

Helen overheard three men drafting a letter for the elders in Eric's living room, so she came from the bedroom and asked, "Why are you here? You turned out to be my husband's enemy instead of his relative. Leave Eric alone. Get out of here!"

Eric's relatives, even his brother Nark, knew about the plan to eliminate Eric, but nobody informed him.

Helen watched them go through the window. One of them said, "Who asked this woman to come home? There is nothing we can do while his wife is home. Eric is now protected. There is no hope; Eric had won again. We must involve Helen."

"Listen," Helen said, "Christ said our enemies are our family members and relatives." They all ran away.

The next day, Eric and Eddie hurriedly drove up to the bank. Hastily, in anger, Eric signed a letter. Eddie hugged Eric and he, too, quickly signed the letter.

Eric looked back, and saw Helen standing behind him. He said, "Helen, a problem came to my attention in the meeting yesterday. The elders have spited themselves. Instead of prolonging a delay, they have merely hastened my intended plan."

Eddie laughed, and said, "Helen, Eric's proposal is the finest. We have already signed the stopped check."

She also laughed, then hugged and kissed Eric.

He went into the bank manager's office. "Sit down," the manager said. Eric said to himself, "Look at the bastard. My education is my weapon. Today is the day."

Outside, Eddie and Helen waited.

Eric handed the letter to the bank manager. He read it and asked, "Stop payment until the bank hears from you, Eric?"

"Yes," said Eric. "Stop the elders from using the community's money to enrich themselves."

The manager shook his head, and said, "I wish the country could have a few more people like you, Eric."

Eddie and Helen sat talking with the bank manager's secretary. Eddie looked over at Eric and the manager, then said, "Over the years since Eric opened the account, there have been plenty of people who disliked him personally, and a few whose antagonisms went deeper, but no one, even in enmity, could reasonably accuse him either of laziness or procrastination. A very good example of Eric's habit of getting things done is the decision he made today."

"Very well said," Helen agreed. "The money is safe now. Eric will sleep."

A few minutes later, a group of ten men rushed into the bank. "Give us our money," Nark said as he handed a check worth $500,000 to the teller. The teller started to reply, then decided against it. After all, he had not gained the victory. Maybe the ten of them would end up in jail.

Soon after, the manager called the police. The ten men were accused. "This is solely a matter of law and order," said the manager. "If you care for some advice, tear the check up quickly before the head of police arrives. Go and call Eric," the manager advised.

The ten men ran away as fast as their legs could carry them, saying, "Today we see what Eric's education can buy. He made fools of the whole community."

The police ran after them until the manager stopped them. One of the community's youths said, "His loyalty and strong sense of duty has kept Eric quiet uptill now, but he's made no secret of wanting to return to private life."

Two years later, Helen and Eric went abroad and never returned to his town. Eric's dynamic and inexhaustible feeling, that he called obligation to his town and relatives became like a dream. Eric recognized the truth that his life had been in danger from continuous threats.

The change brought Eric encouragement and peace of mind, peace in his family, peace with Helen, and peace in the work he loved to do. Helen reclaimed something valuable and precious that she had almost lost. Now Helen had everything she ever wanted, mostly Eric's trust.

She thought, "Why can't I bubble with joy? Oh, there is a smile on Eric's face all right, a smile fixed in place with our determination to build a better marriage. We can be the perfect wife, perfect mother and perfect husband. It's a smile of moving into the upper class. It's a smile that can destroy enemies. It's a smile of beautiful plans to change the wicked." Helen was joyfully amazed.

She said, "Yes, we are now in the hands of God. He is our guide. Life must go on, my husband." She kept telling him, "No worried face anymore."

Eric smiled at Helen.

She continued healing their emotional feelings and replaced the pain with hope and a brighter future. She said, "Eric, a rich and famous lifestyle is at hand. We must trust in the Lord. God will listen."

Helen then looked at Eric, and with a smiling face, she added, "I saw the Lord. He saw me. He knows my troubled heart. He will make me whole. I looked at the Lord and He looked at me. He will never fail me."

Helen never cared for what people said, but trusted in the Lord. Trust and love grew in their lifestyle. They never fought, but worked hard to be rich and famous, waiting for God's blessings.

Helen trusted that her empty life would be filled with blessings from God. For we must ask our Lord, we must knock and the door shall be opened. There are many blessings in the house of our Father. He will bless us in His time and on His terms.

Chapter Twenty

In 1980, a voice said to Helen, "Ask your husband to accept a transfer. Go into business. There you will find your blessings."

Helen said, "Please let me establish my career first."

The voice said again, "Answer me. Who made you? Who has the power to bless and take the little that you have? If you believe I'm the One, follow my direction, follow the voice. Follow the order. No turning back."

She continued battling between her feelings and obedience to the voice, then said, "Yes, business is a part of my university education, but I still want to be more of a professional. Working with people would bring my profession into focus."

Helen really longed to promote her career. She knew that if she entered into business fully, she would speak only business terms and have only business dealings.

The best thing she could do for two years was to combine teaching with working part-time in business.

In 1983, she was discouraged and longed to have her life back, so she obeyed the small voice and went to her father Enoch.

She said, "Daddy, I thought about the possibilities of doing two things at the same time. The more appealing they seem to be, the harder my heart is failing.

"I know you will not like to hear this, but I love being in an office as a working class lady and a businesswoman, but now it is time to choose only one."

Enoch said, "Helen, don't tell me you're quitting your job."

"It's true, Daddy," said Helen. "I noticed, saw and heard the truth, Daddy. It is time to move forward."

Enoch said, "Business has more of a down side. That's going backward. Please don't do that. I'm appealing to you, stop talking about leaving your job."

Helen watched Enoch, then she said, "I always loved facts and figures, Daddy. If I am able to use them well, I can make it fine. Never worry. Women are also found in the business world."

As Helen talked to Enoch, the more she felt her decision was genuinely the best. And her heart was filled with happiness. She said, "It is time to tell our society, education before money. It is time to be rich and famous. It took years and hard work to become well-educated. But anybody can be rich. With God's guidance, you will smile, Daddy."

When Enoch saw Helen smiling, he smiled. He said, "May God help you for your trust and in the choice of your new career."

She smiled again and said, "Bye for now. Your daughter is entering the international business world. You won't regret this, but remember me in your prayers."

The moment of truth arrived. Making smart decisions and judgments were the keys to success. "Do I have the control and confidence to achieve this goal?" Helen wondered. She still had some doubts.

She thought and said, "I may not be able to bear the idea that someone else might disapprove of my choice. If I don't trust my own instincts, I could easily be swayed. Other people's opinions and new information could change my goals."

Helen continued feeling afraid of having too little control of her life. She didn't want to fall into the magical belief that one path is best. She said, "The path could lead to happiness or another misery. One is never sure which is which. To figure out what is the best is the hardest."

Trusting the voice, Helen made the decision to move forward. No turning back.

Helen wrote her desires and dreams in life, her goals as they were relative to the decisions she made. Once again, she identified her wishes and priorities. She prayed, "Lord, give me heart to follow the true voice that asked me to change my career. If that is your voice, the true voice, take charge of my desires and priorities. My progress in life is in your hands, Lord."

Helen gathered as much information as she could and went on her business trip. She started with one of the richest countries. The goods were cleared and stored, and she was happy about her choice.

But a month later, all the customers refused to honor their promises. She couldn't sell her goods; instead, her friends' goods became her major focus. Helen's dreams became nightmares.

At the end of the second month, the voice said, "Give the goods to Eric's friend."

Helen said, "How can I give goods worth $60,000 to a friend?"

"Are you doing it or not?" asked the voice.

"Do I have a choice?" asked Helen.

There wasn't another alternative. As a result of this problem, making another choice became even more difficult for Helen. "There is a key attitude to maintain, but do I have such an attitude?" asked Helen. She listened, waited, and said, "It seems there is temptation behind my decisions."

As time went on, she learned flexibility and how to accept risk. She decided to face the reality of the human world. She reassessed her faith and the future. Helen gave Power Daniel, Eric's friend, the goods.

Six months later, Helen had survived the big disappointment. Eric was involved in the crusade to regain what she had lost. An important decision was on the way. This was the biggest offer Helen ever had.

When the fateful day arrived, Eric rejected a deal already accepted because the customer did not have the money to pay for the goods. Helen said, "Sweet, just allow the man to pay with whatever he has."

Eric said, "An agreement is a contract."

"Please, the goods are already with him," said Helen. Eric was playing with a $250,000 deal.

The man promised to return within two days with the money. Three days later, Eric went to find him. He felt sadness and confusion.

While Eric was away, the children saw Helen crying and praying. She said, "I'm having a nightmare. Is it true again? Am I dreaming? Is someone chasing me or is my luck going bad? I commit my progress into your hands, Lord. I will take all the consequences of my decision."

The voice said, "The man is in jail."

The children said, "We can't understand why and how you allowed Daddy to make decisions over your business deals. He hasn't handled lots of money like you. How can you, mama?"

Helen said, "Easy lessons just don't carry the same weight. Whatever the outcome, Eric has now experienced the business world. My children, the man is in jail. That is his reward for not paying for my goods."

Kate said, "Mama, you already told us if the man brings local money it doesn't matter. The money would buy us a house. Where is our house?" they cried.

Helen said, "The man duped others to pay for my goods. We can't be a party to his evil behavior. Let's wait for God's intervention instead of a prolonged frustration, my children."

She looked at them and said, "I understand, all these years people have been waiting for God's blessing that hasn't happened. But never forget His hands and blessings are very closed because our impossibilities are the platforms upon which He does His best work.

The Lord's delays are not really his denials. God's time doesn't imply His unwillingness to help us. But when He intervenes, His intervention always brings immediate joy and happiness for our ultimate good.

Three months later, Helen found a business partner. They never used any contract but trust.

Eric never understood and never believed how a human being could offer trust like Helen. But he saw it work when Jane Chris, Helen's partner, carried goods worth $50,000 with no down payment and no written agreement.

The evening of the same day, Jane returned with the money and a bottle of red wine. She said, "Helen, your goods always move very fast. Before they arrive at the office, customers are already lining up. Here's your money."

Helen hugged Eric, then said, "Indeed, I'm rejoicing for God's surprise for this is the way the Lord has dealt with me in the days when His favor hour came upon me to take away my disappointments and disgrace among those still waiting for the crown.

Eric stood waiting with his mouth wide open, seeing God's ability to do what he called impossible after many years of failure and rejections in the society of rich. This time Helen was able to have better results from her plans. She had hope, courage and confidence to take up the challenge and follow the commands of the true voice.

Two months later, Kate and Justine, Helen's daughters talked to her and said, "Mama, your business is fine again. We hope daddy is not going to make another foolish decision to make you sad. This family is not ready for more sorrow like the sorrow he caused us."

Helen looked at them, and said, "Come closer, my daughters. This is like what my mama told me. You will soon be women and men. Sit down my children."

"Have we done you wrong?" they asked.

"Oh no, just listen," Helen responded.

Then she said, "My daughters, marriage has magic vision. The man feels he is the head of the home. He makes the final decision."

"No, Mama," they countered.

"You always say marriage is an equal partnership," said Justine.

"That's why he had the right to express his opinion," Helen argued.

"Don't you understand?" they questioned. "Dad didn't express his opinion: he forced his decision on us. He failed us. No man is ever going to make decisions for us. We shall be equal partners in everything, that's what you taught us."

Peace said, "Mama, we remember that Daddy said never to use his name in your business dealings, but you use your daddy's name. 'Never attach my name,' our daddy said."

"Yes, children, I remember," said Helen.

Alice asked, "Who uses the business money? We know Daddy plays a rich man who is proud of his wife's work. But he never gives her a free hand to make her own decisions. Sometimes he feels sad when your business turns out well, because he wasn't party to the deals and the decision making."

Peace said, "We also observe that the business doesn't work well if Daddy is with you. His luck is not for business. Never go on a business trip with him."

"My son, business is a very rough career," said Helen. "There is very little room for relaxation. Well done, children. Eric uses part of the money, but he is not a dictator anymore. He has learned his lessons."

Peace looked, laughed, and hugged Helen, then said, "I hate to see you crying. Please learn to rest and sleep. Daddy sleeps a lot but you don't."

Kate, was in the kitchen cooking dinner, but she was listening to all that was being said. Peace watched and laughed.

"But that is fine, Peace " Helen said. "In the business world, one must plan constantly and make decisions."

Helen continued to teach Peace about the behavior of a father and his relatives. She said, "There is another strong problem, children. Friends, in-laws, and husbands never like a woman having more money than the man."

"Oh no, Mama," they said. "They don't understand Daddy."

"Nobody controls Daddy, but one must have good reasons for him to approve the plans," Helen explained.

"But you're a good planner, Mama," they came back.

Helen said, "When you're married, let your husband make decisions sometimes. He will then understand his own ability. By doing that, he will not hate or fight with you. Let your husband make mistakes." He will learn from his mistakes.

"My daughters," she added, "a man is the head of every home though we are equal partners. Give your husband some room to feel and use his rights. He will seek your help when he fails. He will then respect you."

Peace said, "Mama, when you buy fish and meat, Daddy never stops you. But when you travel, Daddy never allows us to buy fish. He saw Kate pricing fish, and he touched her and said your mama is not home. Do not buy the fish."

Helen laughed and said, "I deal with cash daily. Eric doesn't know how much I sell my goods for unless I tell him. His brother deprived him of that right. But Eric knows what I do with my money."

"What do you do with your money, Mom?" asked Alice. "We want to know."

"Are you ready to see?" Helen also asked .

"Yes, Mama," said Justine. Kate laughed and said, "I know about Mama's plan. One day I shall be like Mama."

Peace said, "Oh, Mama, let's go now before it gets too late."

Helen was enjoying this time with her children. She said, "Excuse me, children, but finally she give me half an hour to wrap up my plans."

Peace later said, "I'm not in a hurry. Mama told me

about her plans last week when I asked. She just wants to wait."

"Oh no, my children," said Helen. "I don't want to walk out right away because it is just nice for all of us to be here," she graciously explained.

Justine said, "Mama, you didn't tell us that you started building a house."

"That's true, my children," Helen replied "The building project started when my business began to improve after Eric stopped controlling and making decisions."

For many years Helen's children anxiously waited and wondered for the great day her search and prayer for blessings would come true. Helen's gracious news overshadowed their fear.

Justine said, "We have been searching for so long for the right words to say." They pulled closer to their mother and effortlessly said, "We love you." They hugged her again and again. Helen kissed and hugged them.

The children said, "We have waited for this for so long. Thank you, Lord. We believed and said that if God is with us, our parents' dream for the family would finally come true. Our hearts were joyfully waiting for God to fulfill our hopes. We can now feel your sincerity in everything. No aching heart. Our heart balloons with love as our eyes watch Mama and Daddy madly in love again."

Helen said, "Remember, this house will give Eric the joy he requires to change his status, our status."

"What do you mean?" Peace asked.

Helen gazed at her children and said, "The man's status is the family's status. It means happiness, excitement, and respect. Eric is now a happy man, so his wife and children are happy also."

"Are you saying once Daddy is happy, the whole family is happy? Are you happy, Mom?" asked Kate.

Helen said, "Look and listen, my daughters. Family values and morality often require female self-sacrifice. But families that exclude women need that required broken woman to hold them together. Such families have built themselves into their own death holes. A woman needs to be creative.

"Sometimes, the pressures of stardom stifle the creative spirit.

"I'm saying that we can't have happy families until we have happy women, women who are well-nurturing of themselves as well as their husbands and children.

"That doesn't mean you're never going to cook and sacrifice anything of yourself for the family. I want all to understand that my pleasure as a mother is important as their pleasure. But, I'm a mother with my own life, too. Women have to take care of themselves. Families have to raise children to know that their mothers are people with other separate needs. Good mothers don't claim and steal children like properties."

Kate got up and served everyone ice cream as Helen continued. "If a son really understands that, if he grows up with a mother who is hardworking, pleasure loving, self-nurturing, and happy with herself, one can imagine the pleasure for the son's future wife and family." The boys laughed.

Helen watched her children, then said, "Remember to make a real effort to show him and her your real self, not only your idealized self." They all opened their eyes wide and looked down.

"Finally, it is necessary to remember what pleases you and do it after marriage. Never let the notion or people's talk that it might be selfish stop you. The moment you start to feel that way, know that you are in danger. Your sexuality and self are at risk. The silence, the secret unhappiness of the woman who has lost pleasure, will poison her whole family."

Kate said, "So Mama must be happy to keep the family together and happy."

"You got it," said Helen.

"Also remember that many women and men of my generation have similar stories to tell, like those I interviewed. It was unusual to hear women and men in the 1940s and '50s speak about their parents."

Helen continued to impart more knowledge to her children. She called it good nurturing and premarital preparation.

"Listen, my loving children." She went on "Many children feel their parents have been essential role models who provided nurturing and support, especially in their development as young men and women. Some may also identify more with their mothers than they do with their fathers.

"But modern women reversed many of the patterns of their mothers. The theme of the twentieth century is that women are behaving like men. They are likely to marry later than men, have children later, have fewer children, then divorce. Also, many women with a university education are living a single life, but they still nurture their children. Being born a woman means nothing to those who see themselves as equal.

"Others identify with their mothers who married young or early. They have children with hardworking experiences. Those whose mothers headed the family, strive to replace their fathers in that role.

What children, mostly females, are fighting for in these modern times is being the first generation of women who really break into male jobs, ranks, and status.

"I watched my own mother's experience working to break down the barrier of just being a good housewife. But I strive to become a good mother, manager, wife and healer," Helen added. "I take after Mama, like Benson said, I'm another in the long chain of a strong family."

★ ★ ★

Helen then chose to reflect on motherhood in modern times.

The role a modern woman searches for most of the time is discovered in adolescence, the most important time of our lives. For Helen, her mother was one of the best role models.

Helen's mother gave her a source of power and strength outside the father. Sometimes we don't understand our mothers when they talk. They understand that we have abilities, talents and the potential to do wonderful things.

Until somebody sees children and recognizes them, they remain unexplored people. Their talent is then wasted.

Mothers are the explorers, teachers and homemakers.

Children are not going to struggle, fight and separate from their mothers. They can listen to their mothers' guiding words without rejecting them out of hand, for their mothers have more experience in this world.

Mothers are often the ones who guide and cheer children on to womanhood and manhood. The better the mother the better the marriages, the families, and the peace in society, the country and the world.

It wasn't until Helen started taking the responsibility of training her children that she fully understood the values of early education.

She began to realize that a woman's role never stops as long as she lives. For the mother is the most important building block in a child's life.

Justine said, "Mama, when I grow up, have a good education, and my own money like you, I shall not manage my husband's income like you do. We will tell stories while I'm cooking, unlike our daddy who sleeps on the sofa."

Through Helen's nurturing, the children became super creative. They could handle a lot of responsibilities. They were articulate and socially skillful. They were ethical, confident, and caring for others.

Good nurturing makes good children, good women or wives, good men or husbands, and good teachers.

Bad nurturing sends children, men and women out to the street to commit crimes.

"We can only change by good nurturing. We can nurture our husbands and wives to produce happy marriages. But remember," said Helen, "I would step in if my child is going to be hurt or hurt others. His or her freedom would then be controlled.

"My children are the best thing that ever happened to me," she continued. "Good nurturing builds trust and truth in children that leads to happiness in later life. That is what you never had, Eric. The unstructured environment motivated you to have affairs with women who were not self-disciplined and educated and who used children only for profit and status.

"I never want my children to act like you, Eric," she continued. "Nurturing parents trust their children's fairness because they themselves have demonstrated fairness and good judgment."

Eric gazed at her and shook his head, even though they had been together for many years and Helen's loyalty was unquestioned.

"Believe me, darling," said Helen, "when a woman plays the role of a man and woman, it means the children have no father role model."

Many people, including their friends, said, "They are in love, those stubborn, crazy, smart people, but why can't she forget everything else and just be with her husband? Sure his wife loves a challenge, but Eric can't resist the lure of other women, and he wants a fortune."

To this Helen replied, "This is what I'm afraid of. Look, darling, your older children are following in their parents' footsteps."

"What are you talking about, Helen?" asked Eric.

"Are you the only stranger in our community?"

"I don't understand what you are talking about."

"Fine, Eric," said Helen. "They are not better, but only lover boys. They listened to my advice because I'm not their mother. They're having babies like you, Eric."

Eric walked closer and said, "I didn't want you to know."

While Helen was on a business trip, Eric drove his sons to their mothers because they never left Helen in peace. Eric sent them away to learn the true secret of man's survival.

Helen then kept to herself and didn't trust anyone. She shunned any silly talk from Eric's relatives blasting her. Many times the children and relatives planned for their divorce, to make Eric suffer. Helen became too tough to handle. The family was never ready to learn and change, but Helen talked about change and made it happen.

Peace and Justine said, "Mama, Daddy can't talk to us because of his past. Like father, like sons. We shall find our way in time."

Helen gazed at Peace and said, "Eric's children from out of wedlock never had good nurturing in their early childhood. Without exception, their mothers were not educated; therefore, they gave them no respect, but were only bossy and controlling.

Eric said, "Helen, you know me. I wasn't a dropout."

"That's true," Helen agreed, "but you know children most of the time follow the wrong track. Are you afraid to reveal that their mothers were prostitutes? You're ashamed, Eric."

Helen then faced Eric and added, "They pick the easiest way out. They entered the world of no morals."

Eric's heart was beating wildly, hoping his past would not be revealed, but Helen said, "Eric, your children deserve to know the facts. Tell them the truth."

But he only became sad and depressed again. A month later, he said, "Helen, I have other children. Though some are girls, I cherish them. Like mother, like daughters. They are my sons."

Eric was not a happy man. The past continued to hurt and haunt him again and again. He was ashamed of his deeds.

Chapter Twenty-One

In 1988, having seen and witnessed his damaged side, Helen decided to find one last healing source. Helen learned her lesson the hard way.

She looked at Eric and thought, "The person with whom we fall in love and marry somehow seems to be able to react to our damaged sides and bring to life that which has long been wounded and dormant. It's agonizing to move the part that is wounded. Surely, his feeling could be restored. But would he appreciate it?

"It's hard to show gratitude when the pain is very deep. But we must remember that we fall in love with the person who needs from us the most difficult thing we can give. We need to give it in order to heal our own inner wounds."

Three days after Helen decided to save and protect Eric from his past hurting, she knelt and prayed. The voice spoke and said, "It is right to forgive him and also right to change him. You can help him, but you can't force him to change because the change is within."

When Eric heard Helen talking, he knelt down and prayed with her, after hearing many people complain that they never saw his car parked there.

He began going to church again and felt peaceful, even with the hardship of his car breaking down everyday because people hit it day and night. Eric trusted God and realized what he was doing. He went through prayer rehabilitation; Helen was his prayer mate.

Eric realized that only through God's grace could he be saved and blessed. He fasted three days a week, asking for forgiveness. He said, "Helen, don't stop healing me."

"If you believe in God, the power of God will make you whole," Helen responded.

Three months later, the voice returned and said, "Helen, you have won your battle. Eric will get a well-paid job."

Helen said, "Eric, the voice came back and told me you will have a good job within two days. The salary won't be less than $30,000. It said, you should continue with the present job until the permanent position is ready."

"Thank you, Lord, my prayer is answered," Helen told the voice.

Eric didn't believe yet. He asked, "Helen how can you know the day, the salary? I heard many words that came from your mouth while sleeping."

"Eric, what you heard came through my mouth but not from me. I believe the message," said Helen. "Eric, never be afraid. Remember what happened to your friends since 1974? Never forget the mysterious fire, set up to burn our children in 1968, and the miraculous recovery after the fire."

Eric said, "Yes, you have been used to achieve wonderful things, but the salary and date? I can't believe what I'm hearing."

"Eric, just wait to see the power of God. Have faith, Eric," she assured him.

Eric told Benson the unbelievable news.

About 2:00 p.m, the second day, the voice said, "Helen, a visitor is waiting. Go home now."

Reaching the gate, Helen saw a stranger's car. She opened the gate and entered the living room. She was not surprised because she trusted the voice's message.

Richard Kingsley, a personnel officer, asked, "Are you Mrs. Eric?"

"What can I do for you, Mister. Kingsley?" Helen asked. "Please sit down."

Kingsley wondered and said to himself, "Is she the woman? "

Helen asked again, "Why are you here?"

Richard said, "We have been looking and waiting for Eric. He's not in the office."

Helen wasn't embarrassed to hear Eric wasn't in his office, but she asked, "Not in the office?"

"Yes, nobody saw him since this morning," Richard replied.

She looked at Richard and said, "Maybe his car is in the garage."

After one hour of waiting and talking, Richard said, "I think we can do the right thing." Then Richard interviewed Helen for the position for Eric. He looked at Helen and said, "It's true, Eric is in good hands. Tell him to come and sign a contract. He is offered a one-year contract until he can free himself from his present job."

Helen looked at Kingsley with a smile on her face. "Thank you," she said.

Kingsley said, "Surely you're full of surprises. Eric's boss who knows you very well, told us not to worry, that if we meet his wife, we've already met Eric. If we discuss with you, we have discussed with Eric. She will surprise you, his boss told us."

Helen laughed and said, "Oh, Eric's boss saw you. He knows we are very close. He also knows me very well."

"You are really a wonderful lady and a valuable asset to Eric's progress," said Richard. "Not many women can have their husband's interests in mind and so dearly in their hearts."

Helen responded, "That's a wife's share of labor, to promote progress and harmony. A woman who isn't proud of her husband's progress and denies him her support isn't fit to marry. Husband and wife must support each other to fulfill the purpose in the creation of woman."

"Hold on, Kingsley," said Helen. "my husband must be on his way. He is probably held up with the traffic."

"We have spent three hours already," said Kingsley. "I must go now."

Just before the driver pulled out of the gate, Eric honked his car horn, and Helen jumped outside. "Here is the lucky man," said Kingsley. "He is here."

"Yes, here is my husband," said Helen.

Eric signed the contract, and Kingsley said, "Eric you are one of the luckiest men on this planet. You have a lovely wife. Never forget her. She's your backbone."

The next day, Eric's boss told Kingsley, "I'm the head of this department. We got Eric here through his wife. She made the deal for him and promised to keep his promise. The man kept her promise. They are two in one. She is really in love with Eric."

"Some men are very lucky," said Kingsley.

Eric, Benson and Power were shocked and intimidated by their little faith. They said, "Truly God is with you, Helen." They continued to ask, "How did you know the salary? Who told you?" She never said a word, but laughed three times.

Eric, Benson, and Power again started going to church with Helen. Benson said, "Yes, we have seen the power of God. Yes, God can answer our prayers."

Helen devoted herself to saving, protecting and building Eric's status as well as the family's status through prayer, fasting, and true love.

Seven days later, the voice said, "Helen, the job is hard, but you can win."

Helen followed the order and command of the voice again. She never went on another business trip without strong prayer and response.

Chapter Twenty-Two

Three years later, Helen succeeded in completing the building of a beautiful modern house, which truly represented Eric's status in society. It was so modern, that people came from different parts of the state to see it, modern enough to make the elders call Eric number one. It was modern enough to feel the work of God, modern enough to promote love, intimacy and the couple's commitment to each other. It was modern enough to create an atmosphere of security and stability, modern enough to prove a woman is not born poor and a slave. It was modern enough to prove that money is much easier to get than education. It takes brains to be well-educated.

Helen praised the Lord for his blessings and kindness., saying, "Thank you, Lord. Eric is not going to sit on the floor any more during town meetings. Thank you for all your blessings, mostly our health, our house and our children's education. Glory be to your name, Lord."

In November of 1989, so many congratulating letters arrived that Eric couldn't believe what he saw. Eric dressed perfectly in a native wrapper and sat on a chair.

Many friends and relatives came for enjoyment. He became rich and famous, he was then called Doctor Eric.

Eric looked great and very happy, but he never forgot who changed his life. He said, "I was an ordinary man who had nothing more to offer than my education. For ten good years, my mind and heart have been burning with tears. I sulked in my bed, miserable, and unconsciously ignored my wife and children

"For ten years, I thought I would die because I was nobody compared to my friends," then joyfully said, 'Oh Lord, I naively drifted away out of your sight and out of my self-control. Take me back. Take me home, Lord.'"

Eric continued, "Who would have Helen and not be proud? She is my pride. I'm back home again for good. The old Eric is gone. I'm new, Lord."

His friends said, "You have a right to be happy, Eric. You are a lucky man. We do envy you. Helen is too good. You owe her your life."

Eric looked at them and said, "I have a life now. I was dead, but now I live again." He said to his sister, Darcy, "Helen's money built this house. She made me a man in this society. That is the truth. You have known the truth. Today you witness the truth Darcy."

Darcy walked around the house with a smile on her face, then said, "Brother, now I can stand before the elders to shout your name. Finally, brother, you have enough to be proud of. I now feel you are worthy." She shouted, "Shut your mouth, whoever says bad things about my brother. This is Eric's ground."

"Everyone can now understand the real truth behind our marriage. We can't change destiny. From now on, I understand we are born to be one flesh. Maybe we shall leave this world together as partners."

Eric smiled and shouted, "Thank you, Lord! Open my mind and heart that I may feel your presence daily." He hugged Helen and said, "I love you forever."

Helen gazed at Eric and sang a song:

I saw the Lord, and He saw me,
I cried to the Lord, and he heard me,
He called me, and I heard his voice,
I said, Lord send me, I will go, I will go.
Yes, I will follow the true voice,
Yes, Lord, I will follow, follow, follow the true voice.

Eric watched Helen as she ended the song, then he hugged her again. and said, "Thank you for making this marriage possible. Only in your arms do I come alive. I'm alive again, darling."

His voice started to whisper, "I love you, you love me, we will always be together."

Helen said, "Lord, I'm waiting for your call. I'm ready and waiting."

Chapter Twenty-Three

For many years, Enoch wanted to see Helen's children. The last time Helen visited Enoch was three years earlier, he said, "The next time you visit, bring your children, Helen."

Helen said, "Enoch, you never loved me. How can you love my children? We are women, not your favorites." She continued wondering, Why this sudden change for love? He never nurtured me. How can he nurture my children? Helen searched for an explanation of his new desire to see her children.

Enoch felt lonely inside without Helen's children, so he asked "Helen, do you remember, during one of your visits you told me about the help your children rendered to complete my house? I gradually eased into a relaxed state of mind, and slowly my dreams focused on their love, giving me sweet dreams."

Helen laughed and said, "My children are far away, but okay, Dad. We have to save for their coming home during the holidays."

Enoch continued, "You know, Helen, I listened to their slow, soft voices in dreams. I became tense trying to see them in real life.

"When your sister Judy came for fish, I said, 'Please Judy, I need to see Helen's children. I am hungry to see them. Help me. Try to advise Helen to bring her children home. I can't relax." Enoch continued to repeat some focused words, mainly that they would be a good gift for Christmas.

Enoch's feelings became very stressful, testing Judy's right to act on his behalf on account of his old age. He was 102 years old.

Judy called her first three children, she bought a live chicken and sent it with them to Enoch's house. She quietly said, "Ask Daddy to bless you, my children. He will forget Helen's children after eating the chicken."

Arriving at Enoch's house, they said, "Granddaddy, your stress will soon heal. Take this chicken for the Christmas meal. Mama said you very much want to talk to us."

But in her effort to gain more blessings for her children, Judy forgot that Enoch could still have Helen's children on his mind. Enoch said, "Oh, Judy, this is like the Bible story of Jacob and Esau. I can still recognize Helen's children, and you are still a jealous sister. You have been with me all these years, but you can't be faithful like her." Then they roasted the chicken and ate the Christmas meal.

As Enoch told the story, Helen said, "Oh, Judy, you can't always be jealous. The world is hungry for people like you to change."

When Judy walked in and looked at her, Helen said, "Sister, open your eyes and see the light. Light and darkness can't be together. You can't change my destiny."

Judy started crying and hugged Helen. Helen said, "Yes, I am a woman, Daddy. I have done what a man can do for you. One day you will bitterly answer for how you rejected me because I was born a woman."

Enoch turned his back and left the room.

Helen and Judy remembered how they labor and nurtured their brothers, These brothers became very stubborn and called Judy and Helen names. They behaved and tried to be the lords of the family, claiming rights, forgetting how Helen and Judy had trained them.

Helen and Judy watched Enoch sleeping in his bed, and they said, "Daughters are the head of your family. God gave us this right. With this stunning announcement, they felt proud of being woman.

Helen never accepted their manish control role. She said, "Benson, a mature man must face life as it strikes, make decisions and consider other options." She always called them baby brothers because they feared criticism. They never fully lived the manly role they claimed.

Helen never wanted to respect a man's interest without roleplaying. A lazy man never excited her. Their little tricks and surprises never tempted Helen to give up her rights.

Benson said, "A man is a man. He is the head of every family."

Helen laughed and said, "A man who can't defend the family is not a man. Such a man is less than a woman." Helen and Judy continued their roleplaying and support.

"The elders and society make women weak. We cannot let that continue," said Helen. "Women before and after us recognized that separate jobs separate man and woman, not just their sex organs. The two work together because two brains are better than one. Husband and wife make a unit."

When Benson was thirty years old, he said, "Helen, you are a woman. You are under me," though I'm in need of $100 for a party.

Helen said, "How refreshing your request, action and command. "No, Benson. Even my husband never felt and said that to me. He never controlled me, Benson. God controls me, not you. My husband and my mom are the only two people who have that right, but even they never controlled me. I am an equal partner with Eric, my husband."

"Helen, you will soon beg me for help," Benson warned. "You are a woman." He shouted at her, beating the table without showing respect for Helen. His threat kept spreading farther and farther into her brain.

"That's pretty silly, baby brother Benson," Helen chastized.

"You should stay on the trail, pumping hands, kissing women and selling your unpopularity in my house."

Benson continued, "Not long from now you will kneel to beg me for help. You are a woman. A son is the head of every family. I'm the head and there's nothing you can do."

"That's your dream," Helen childed. She tried to ignore him, but he didn't stop, so Helen said, "You're abusing me just because I have no money for your party." Besides your reaction, when are you going to focus on self reliance.

Helen's brothers-in-law stood watching, so she looked at them, and said, "Yes, I am a woman. But God will never punish me for being good to Enoch's children, the so-called sons."

Eric was very disappointed. He became so angry and frustrated that he nearly drove Benson out. He said, "Benson, your sister loves you and still wants to continue your training until you get your diploma. But listen very carefully, Benson: you see Helen as only a woman, but we never see her as only a woman. Tell us, what can a man of our age and time do that Helen has not done? In this society, Benson, you are a woman."

Eric continued to lecture Benson., sayings, "Do you know your mother? Who cared for you and trained you? You're aware of what your sisters have done for you. You're a man without a portfolio. You're the woman and people are laughing at you."

Eric then said, "Unless I'm dead, my wife will never beg you for help. Even after my death, I have faith in her future without you. Benson, you are one of the bad brothers."

Benson stood without saying a word. He had never seen Eric so angry before and he was dismayed.

Eric shouted and said, "Benson, we understand that Enoch wanted a son at the time he had Helen. What have you done in this world without the support of your two sisters? The so-called sons. No, no, you're a damn ingrate."

Helen laughed and said, "I don't remember you collecting walnuts with Judy and me. That was how we fed you, Benson, until we put ourselves through school. You're now collecting your own walnuts."

Benson became silent and ashamed.

Eric said, "Look at me. Tell us the difference."

Helen murmured and felt a wondrous relief to hear Eric say that just being a man is not the answer. She said, "Oh, boy, if you only knew how we grew up, you would thank your sisters and God that we were born women."

Enoch died at the age of 103. Benson phoned and said, "It has happened, the old man is gone. Daddy is dead. Come home and bring a lot of money. You know our culture. Daddy was a very old man."

Helen said, "I'm just a woman. What of the head of the family? I'm just a woman, Benson. Bury your father yourself."

He begged for money so much that Helen and Judy could not stand the shame. They said, "You are a jealous wreck. Bury your father, baby brother. We're just women."

Because Helen and Judy were the major breadwinners of the family, in the end they took care of Enoch's funeral. He received a Christian burial followed by a large party.

The sons Enoch called the new generation were still behind the times. The old man died without any love and care from his sons.

Enoch never challenged the creation of God. A man and a woman are creations of God. Hopefully, men will someday accept this equality because we are all equal in the sight of God.

Chapter Twenty-Four

Seven months after Enoch's death, Helen saw herself in a dream. She saw Rebecca and Enoch, and she stood watching them talking. Enoch said, "Please Rebecca, let me come over and join you, please."

Rebecca answered and said, "Oh no, Enoch, you can't cross the bridge between us. We can only talk. You can hear me but can't see me." Enoch was very sad and weary.

Helen woke up with smiles of joy. This gave Helen hope for tracing her adult fears and anxieties back to her childhood's traumatic events. She said, "Oh mama, your kindness and love automatically place you above Enoch.

She rejoiced in a very dramatic way. As Helen recalls, her shouts of joy were trapped in silence. Finally, she remembered looking at Enoch inside the wet, soft, sticky earth holding up his hands, begging Rebecca for mercy.

A shock wave of whisper appeared on Helen's cheek, replacing peace in place of fear, freedom instead of bondage.

"Oh Mama," Helen said, "When God sows his mercy praise blossom in our lives, it becomes a timely principle to bring relief and the God Mercy helps us rejoice the peace and salvation from my childhood abandonment."

Helen envisioned the role of Enoch, and said, "Fatherly pride has burned Enoch's soul into darkness and the everlasting shadow of death. You can't change in the grave Daddy and Mama can't welcome your soul. God's plan is the quick sketch of how you now draw our attention.

"I must continue to try to finish my work," said Helen. "One day, by God's grace, I will finish it, and Mama would welcome me. There isn't fear in me anymore because mama is happy. This is all that remains of my childhood memories.

"It is high time for society to change," Helen continued. "Women, don't be disappointed because being a woman deprived you of your parental love. Never be sad because you have daughters, but pray for their good health and progress to care for them.

"Children, once you are born into this world, carry your cross to build your life. Tomorrow, you will be proud of your achievements and be a role model to others like you. Our daily question is: Is woman a creation of God? Are only men created to be rich and famous?

"We must try. Without trying, we cannot see the good work of our Creator. Yes, I love being born a woman," said Helen. "Those women who have made it are our role models.

"One thing still remains. That a woman has a major role in a man's life. Women shouldn't deny men that role in their lives. Rather, women and men should work hard to complete and fulfill both roles of God's Creation. Once a man and a woman learn to be one body, not separate bodies, they can see with eyes of faith. There will be peace.

"Yes, I love being born a woman," Helen concluded firmly and proudly.

Helen sang a song

When God made a man
He saw it was good
Then He made a woman and
This completed the unit
Together the two are one flesh
Together the two are one body
Together the two are one flesh
Love and peace for all

Come together my friends
Come together my sisters
Come together my parents
Come together my brothers
Come together the world
Then love and peace can spread

Come together
Come together   2 times
Come together
Then love and peace can spread.

Wa ku oma gbo ome
Wa ku oma gbo ome   2 times
Wa ku oma gbo ome
Mare unu va jiri Oghene mai